THE DEADLY MIND-FORCE

I held onto Tarani's squirming body with some difficulty. The fur on the back of my neck and on my hands stood on end. Something was building inside Tarani, a kind of pure thought-energy that seemed to reach out to touch my mind, which recoiled as if it had been singed. Out of the corner of my eye, I saw Yayshah surge to her paws, her eyes wild, the fur around her neck rippling out.

"Get away," Tarani said, her voi̶̶ ̶̶fled against my shoulder. "Please, darling, get̶ ̶̶ ̶̶me! *I don't want to hurt you!*"

Tarani screamed. Sear̶̶ ̶̶st forth from her. It was as th̶̶ ̶̶ad lived through had been ga̶̶ ̶̶illed to the essence of exper̶̶ ̶̶with Tarani's power of illusi̶̶ ̶̶e giant whine.

It was insta̶̶

It was devast̶̶

I blacked out .̶̶

Praise for *The Gandalara Cycle* by
Randall Garrett & Vicki Ann Heydron:

"Excellent sf/fantasy . . . The places are beautifully described and the characters are vivid. I look forward to the rest!"

—Faren Miller, *Locus*

"Entertaining and well paced . . . Full of swordplay and giant cats."

—Theodore Sturgeon,
The Twilight Zone Magazine

THE GANDALARA CYCLE

V

THE SEARCH FOR KÄ

RANDALL GARRETT and VICKI ANN HEYDRON

BANTAM BOOKS
TORONTO • NEW YORK • LONDON • SYDNEY • AUCKLAND

THE SEARCH FOR KĀ
A Bantam Book / August 1984

Map by Robert A. Sabuda

ISBN 0-553-24120-6

Published simultaneously in the United States and Canada

Bantam Books are published by Bantam Books, Inc. Its trademark,
consisting of the words "Bantam Books" and the portrayal of a
rooster, is Registered in U.S. Patent and Trademark Office and in
other countries. Marca Registrada. Bantam Books, Inc., 666 Fifth
Avenue, New York, New York 10103.

PRINTED IN THE UNITED STATES OF AMERICA

H   0 9 8 7 6 5 4 3 2 1

THE BRONZE OF EDDARTA

I greet thee in the name of the new Kingdom.

From chaos have we created order.
From strife have we enabled peace.
From greed have we encouraged sharing.

Not I alone, but the Sharith have done this.
Not we alone, but the Ra'ira has done this.

THESE ARE THE WEAPONS
OF WHICH I GIVE THEE CHARGE
AND WARNING:

The Sharith are our visible strength—

Offer them respect;
Be ever worthy of their loyalty.

The Ra'ira is our secret wisdom—

Seek out the discontented;
Give them answer, not penalty.

THIS IS THE TASK I GIVE THEE
AS FIRST DUTY:

As you read the scholar's meaning
Within the craftsman's skill,
So read within yourself
Your commitment

To guide
To lead
To learn
To protect.

If you lack a high need
To improve life for all men,
Then turn aside now,
For you would fail the Kingdom.

I greet thee in the name of the new Kingdom,
And I charge thee: care for it well.

I am Zanek,
King of Gandalara

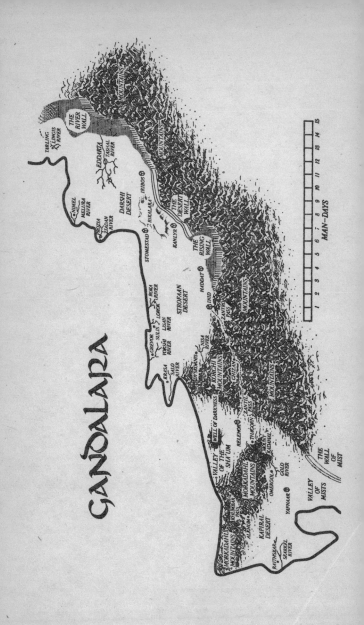

PRELIMINARY PROCEEDINGS:
INPUT SESSION FIVE

—*I didn't mean to startle you, Recorder.*

—*Forgive my surprise. I hear the festival proceeding. Is your participation not required?*

—*It was, but for now my part is done, and I had no interest in seeing the rest of it.*

—*Is that anger I hear in your voice?*

—*Less anger, I think, than exasperation. The story is changed, again. Only a little more than last year, but by that small amount it is less true.*

—*People will always prefer the story they hear from their friends to the one which must be retrieved from the All-Mind by a Recorder. And a story changes in the telling. It is the process by which history becomes legend.*

—*I understand that, Recorder, and I might as well try to stop an angry sha'um as try to reverse the process. But actually witnessing it reminded me that I have been neglecting the task I set myself, that of placing the truth as I know it into the All-Mind. If it is convenient for you now, I would like to continue the Record.*

—*Of course. Please, make yourself comfortable.*

—*What about you, Recorder? Why aren't you celebrating outside with the others?*

—*I have shared your truth. Like you, I have no need to hear it retold as legend. I think, too, that only the time*

1

of your arrival was a surprise. I felt that you would require this service of me today.

—"Require?" Never, Recorder. Request, yes. I have good reason to respect your skill and appreciate its value. If the time is not convenient . . .

—I have said that it is. If you wish to Record, you must first calm yourself. Neither the All-Mind nor I, as its channel, will be able to accept your thoughts smoothly if they are not more ordered than your outward restlessness would indicate.

—I apologize, Recorder. I suppose I am anticipating this session. The concentration required is so complete that it feels very much like reliving the experiences as we are Recording. And the very act of making a Record reminds me . . .

—You are speaking, now, of the tale not yet Recorded?

—Yes.

—Then wait for the telling of it. For now, relax and listen while I prepare myself by recalling the scene which was last Recorded. You and Tarani had, once again, fled Eddarta. You were forced to leave behind the Ra'ira, but you have reason to suspect that it is safe from misuse because Tarani reported that her brother Indomel was having little success in learning its use. You plan to find the ancient city of Kä and retrieve a potent historical symbol, a sword which is the twin to Rika, both swords made of the rare metal, rakor. With the second sword as a talisman, you believe that Tarani can win the support of the other Lords, and take her place as Eddarta's High Lord.

—That was Tarani's only goal, Recorder. I had a different reason for searching for the sword. I knew that Tarani, like me, was a blend of a human and a Gandalaran, except that in her case, both personalities were active. I believed that Tarani, who seemed consciously unaware of Antonia, would achieve integration through the same sort of medium which had turned me

2

into the blended individual called Rikardon. Rika had been my catalyst; I believed that the other sword would work for Tarani.

—But she knew nothing of this other goal.

—No. To tell her would have meant exposing what I thought of as my betrayal, a lack of total honesty between us. We had achieved a physical and emotional closeness that I treasured above all things.

—So we resume now with you and Tarani leaving the Valley of the Sha'um with Keeshah and his mate, who violates all history and instinct by leaving the Valley. Recall your feelings and thoughts at that time . . . good. Now make your mind one with mine, as I have made mine one with the All-Mind. . . .

WE BEGIN!

1

"You were right," Tarani conceded, when we had ridden well out of the Valley of the Sha'um. "It appears that Worfit has not chosen to wait for us."

"More accurately," I said, "his *men* gave up—I doubt that Worfit has quit his hunt for me, or that he ever will."

Tarani stretched forward to stroke the fur along Yayshah's lower jaw. The gray-and-brown brindled sha'um slowed, and pressed her cheek into Tarani's hand.

I watched the cat's eyes shut and the girl's expression change as they slipped into mindlink communication. For Keeshah and me, who had formed our link when the huge tan cat had been a year-cub and the Gandalaran body I was wearing had been twelve years old, the flow of conscious thought between our minds was nearly second nature. Tarani and Yayshah, both fully adult, had formed their link only recently. For them, communicating took special, conscious effort—but I could see that it was becoming easier.

Tarani's face lost that distracted look, and she smiled at me with some embarrassment. "Forgive me," she said. "It is only that Yayshah—when we speak—"

The sha'um were walking, taking it easy by inclination and on my orders, so that Tarani and I were riding in a position more upright than usual, one much closer to a conventional sitting pose. I reached across the distance between the cats and took Tarani's hand in mine.

"When you talk to Yayshah, what is it like?" I asked.

"It is very different from the way Lonna and I communicated," she said.

A shadow passed over her face at the mention of Lonna. The big white bird had helped us through some tight spots, and had seemed to be genuinely fond of me. But I only *missed* Lonna; Tarani had *lost* her. The bird had been her friend and companion for years, the inspiration of Tarani's dream to have her own entertainment troupe, and one of its stars. Not even the magic of a sha'um's friendship could replace what Tarani and Lonna had shared.

"Lonna gave me images," Tarani continued. "Yayshah speaks in *impressions*—do you understand what I mean?"

"I think so," I answered. "Not just a picture, but what she feels about it—fear or contentment, or whatever?"

"Exactly," Tarani agreed. "And she is trying to use— well, not *words* . . ."

"Conversation," I supplied, "is a deliberate attempt to convey or solicit ideas—the most sophisticated use of language. Language is only a code; you can think of a word as a unit of *information*. The direct contact with the sha'um makes the code unnecessary. Keeshah and Yayshah use units of *meaning*."

Tarani was staring at me, the dark eyes looking extraordinarily large in the pale and delicate contours of her face, made more angular by the loss of every unnecessary ounce of weight. I wondered, fleetingly, if the past few weeks of protracted physical effort showed so clearly in my body.

"You continue to surprise me, Rikardon," Tarani said. "The way you speak of contact with the sha'um—"

"Is it different for you and Yayshah?"

"Not at all," she said. "Your description is precise— but not, I feel sure, the product of a sudden insight. You

6

have thought much about the nature of communication, have you not? To what purpose?"

What have I done? I wondered, mentally trying to shake myself alert. *She asked Rikardon a question and Ricardo, the language professor, answered her. I slipped right into my old "lecture mode"—a mannerism totally foreign to Markasset and, until now, to Rikardon.*

"Talking with a sha'um is fairly new to me, too," I said, "even though Markasset had been doing it for years before I arrived. I've never been able to take it for granted—I've thought about it a lot, that's all," I finished lamely.

"I do forget that you are a Visitor," Tarani said, referring to a situation in which a surviving personality returned from the Gandalaran All-Mind to the body of a living person. Apparently this had been a rare but documented occurrence in Gandalaran history, and I had allowed my friends to believe I was such a case. "You have told me little of your earlier life—do you remember it clearly?"

"Yes," I answered, then groaned inwardly.

Wrong answer, I thought. *Now she'll be curious, and I'll have to dodge around the truth—that I come from a completely different world. I might be able to hide it without actually lying, but she'll pick up on the fact that I was "covering up," the way she detected the "professor" in me. And if I had to lie outright, then I'd have to remember which lies I'd told—I can't let that get started.*

I must have been wearing my discomfort on my sleeve because Tarani said: "I will not ask of the past now. One day, perhaps?"

I nodded. She smiled, and squeezed my hand lightly before she let it go and lay forward across Yayshah's back, slipping into mental contact with the sha'um.

I felt awful, as though I had broken my mother's favorite vase, then hidden the pieces in the trash, hoping she wouldn't notice.

I wish I could just tell her who and what I really am, I

thought. *But I just don't know how it would affect her. I'm reminded of a scene from* Anna and the King, *in which a fracas starts because an educated teacher shows the royal children a map with Siam represented in its true proportion to the rest of the world. Tarani doesn't even know there is more to her world, much less that other worlds exist. The Gandalaran cloud cover has blocked the speculation of the nature of the universe that started in Ricardo's world the first time a man saw a star.*

She found it difficult to understand why someone would want to study language—because hers is nearly homogeneous, as unquestioned a fixture of her life as the impassable mountains she calls "Walls." How much harder will it be for her to accept the idea that Gandalara—which seems to me to be two humongous valleys which, placed end to end, are no more than sixteen hundred miles long—has to be only a fraction of the land area on this planet?

But "culture shock" isn't the only reason I'm reluctant, I admitted to myself.

Tarani lay with her cheek pressed against Yayshah's back, just behind the cat's shoulder. Her eyes were closed, and the look of distraction was fading, the muscles of her face relaxing as she dozed off. Awake, Tarani was a formidable woman, strong and competent. Asleep, she looked even younger than her twenty years, thin rather than slim, touchingly vulnerable.

Our relationship exists on many levels, I thought. *We have fought the same enemies and lain together, sharing battle and passion and what we have come to believe is our destiny. The one thing we haven't shared equally is the truth about our pasts.*

Tarani told me about her "arrangement" with Molik under duress, before she really knew me, but the fact remains that I do know how she earned the money to put together that show. She thought that her dancing was all she ever wanted, and worth using her illusion power to help satisfy the roguelord's lust. But that earlier rela-

tionship was still affecting her when I met her. It wasn't until we faced Molik, and she admitted the shame was more in her perception than in her actions that she was able to forgive him and herself, and be free.

Free of the shame, I corrected myself, *but not of the memory.*

She was occupied at that time with worry over Volitar, the man she had known as her uncle, and whom Molik had kidnapped—to coerce Tarani into helping a pair of assassins he was sending after the Lieutenant of the Sharith. When Molik (thanks to Thymas), Volitar (thanks to Gharlas) and Tarani's show (her own choice) were all dead, the girl's past was still with her.

I think that some of Tarani's feeling of "destiny" can be attributed to her need to have some new direction in her life. She came with me, partly, in order to leave behind her past.

That's why I can't bring myself to tell her the truth about Ricardo and Markasset, I realized. *It's not only that she has trusted me, and that I've been lying by evasion whenever we've discussed my "dual" nature. If I tell her about Ricardo, I can't see any way not to tell her about Antonia, too—and that troubled period that centered around Molik will come sharply into focus again, with a slightly different perspective.*

Antonia Alderuccio had been with Ricardo Carillo on the deck of that cruise ship when the meteor—or whatever it was—had hit us. She had been a recent acquaintance, and I had been so occupied in Gandalara that I had given her little thought, except to regret that someone so lovely and charming had been lost. It hadn't occurred to me that she might have come to Gandalara, too—until I had heard Tarani, in a moment of distracted passion, pronounce my name "Ricardo." A man's name without a consonant ending is totally alien to Tarani's culture. I had realized, then, that Antonia had come into this world four years earlier, objective time, and in a different way.

I had occupied a body whose Gandalaran personality had recently died; Antonia had been forced to share her "host" with a live, native personality.

I'm absolutely convinced that it was Antonia who taught a sweet and sheltered sixteen-year-old girl the power of her body, and showed her how to use it. I'm also sure that Antonia has only meant to help the Gandalaran girl. Except for intensifying the conflict between control and helplessness that all adolescents suffer, Antonia's worldliness and maturity have generally been assets to Tarani. The human presence gave Tarani the same protection from Gandalara's mindpower that I have—a dualness that isn't subject to a uniquely Gandalaran force. But Antonia's undetected influence has brought a great deal of confusion and distress into Tarani's life.

Tarani and I have talked about the fact that two people such as we are needed, right here and right now, to keep anyone—least of all her cruel brother Indomel—from using the Ra'ira's power as a telepathic channel to tyrannize and, ultimately, destroy Gandalara. Ricardo and Antonia, it seems, are equally part of that destiny. I can't help being afraid that, once Tarani knows the truth, I'll be linked with that past she's trying to avoid, and—I shuddered—and she'll run from me, just as she runs from her past now.

I'd lose her, I thought. Them. Tarani and Antonia. I love them both, with passion, respect, protectiveness, tenderness, humility—with a magnitude neither Ricardo nor Markasset ever experienced.

When we find the sword—please, God, let that sword be the agent of their union.

I realized that I was actually and sincerely praying—the first time in a long while. And I was a trifle embarrassed to realize that what I was *really* praying for was what Ricardo would have called a "cop-out."

I want the union between Tarani and Antonia to do my explaining for me, I realized. I want Tarani to under-

*stand and forgive, all in one blinding flash of compre-
hension.*

I sighed.

*It would be nice to be able to talk to Tarani without
having to hide anything. Right now, no one knows the
truth—*

I know.

I jumped when Keeshah's thought touched my mind.
The feel of his fur under my hands and his body between
my legs brought me vividly back to reality.

How is it, Keeshah, I asked, when I had recovered
from my shock, **that you can follow my thoughts
without my knowing it, but I have to ask what you're
thinking?**

I was referring to our conscious conversation, not the
rare moments in which he and I merged so completely
that we could share one another's sensory perception.

You think more, he said.

I laughed aloud, remembering at the last second to
muffle the noise so that I wouldn't wake Tarani. Yayshah
looked around at me, her eyes slitted and her ears
cocked back warily, then returned her attention to the
route we were taking.

We had left behind the thick, tangled greenery that
characterized the Valley of the Sha'um—although, strictly speaking, the area was less a valley than the verdant
foothills at the junction of two mountain ranges. The
Morkadahls ran roughly north and south, and another
range of high mountains, which formed part of what the
Gandalarans called the Great Wall, ran roughly east and
west. I guessed there must have been a network of small
streams trickling down from the higher ground, and
probably a sort of underground delta effect, to support
the lushness of the Valley.

We were traveling south, following the eastern edge of
the Morkadahls. The countryside here was much like
what I had seen on the western side of the range—
twisted and curling dakathrenil trees mixed with lots of

species of bushes. Unlike the towering forest that marked the home of the sha'um, few of these plants grew more than six feet high, preferring to cling to and shade the water-giving ground and, in the process, provide homes for the variety of small animals, insects and birds that shared their space.

Moving across the overgrown ground should have been little problem for the sha'um, who were accustomed to the much taller, more complicated, and occasionally barbed undergrowth of the Valley. But I could see that Yayshah was moving with exaggerated caution, placing her feet carefully.

She's having a harder time than you are, Keeshah, I said. *Is it because of her cubs? Is it hurting her to travel?*

Don't know, the cat replied.

There was an overtone of worry in Keeshah's mind, and something more. I felt a sudden sense of alarm.

What's bothering you? I asked him.

Female here because of me. Cubs. Afraid. Don't want hurt.

Don't take all that blame on yourself, I said gently. *Yayshah came along because of Tarani, too—because she can talk to Tarani the same way you can talk to me.*

I felt a sense of agreement from him. *Woman knows what female needs. I don't.*

There was sadness and guilt in the thought, guilt I was forced to share. Keeshah had been deeply enthralled in a period of his life which excluded me, a time when he had been totally preoccupied with the biological need to mate and reproduce. In order to achieve perfect communion with those needs, he had instinctively cut off the conscious functioning of our mindlink. He had been mate and father only, totally devoted to Yayshah.

Tarani and I had been cornered near the poison-filled volcanic crater the Gandalarans called the Well of Darkness. In desperation, I had called to Keeshah. Nothing short of imminent physical danger to me could have penetrated that instinctive blockage, I was sure—but Keeshah's devotion to me had let him re-establish our conscious link, and he had come to us. His presence had saved our lives.

Once he had broken it, Keeshah had not been able to achieve again the natural communion he had forsaken. Yet his loyalty to his family was still in operation, making him feel selfish and concerned that his preference for me would interfere with their welfare.

I know it troubles you that you can't take care of Yayshah the way you think you should, I told Keeshah.

But look at it this way—there are three of us now who love her. We won't let her or the cubs come to any harm.

2

When Tarani awoke, I asked her about Yayshah's caution.

"She moves easily," Tarani said, after slipping into and out of a quick linkage with the female sha'um. "And I sense only a little discomfort because of the cubs. But her eyes seem to be hurting—I think the light hurts her eyes."

"Of course," I said. "The Valley is shady and relatively cool—she must be suffering from all this light and heat." I looked up at the sky which was, as usual, smoky gray with the cloud cover. I didn't have to gauge the position of the brighter spot that marked the sun to tell that it was mid-afternoon; my Gandalaran inner awareness operated like a perpetual clock.

"Let's stop here and rest," I suggested. "We can move on after dark, if we feel like it—it will be easier traveling for Yayshah."

We found a spot between two tall boulders that was relatively shady. Yayshah snuggled down until she was both *on* and *in* the bushy growth at their feet, and went promptly to sleep.

Hunt, Keeshah told me, and bounded away, headed for the higher hills.

"Keeshah's concerned about Yayshah," I told Tarani, as we rearranged some vegetation to make a comfortable resting spot beside one of the big boulders. "Can you tell me how long it will be before the cubs are born?"

Tarani opened her backpack, dipped her hands in, and brought them out full of berries. She tipped one handful into my cupped hands and shook her head.

"I truly do not know, Rikardon," she said. "If Yayshah were still in the Valley, *she* would know, probably down to the very minute. It would be . . . *natural* for her."

Natural? I wondered. *Meaning instinct? Or simply the same sort of inner awareness as the people have? That would mean that the sha'um have their own equivalent of an All-Mind. Not surprising, I thought. The very fact that sha'um can link with men and communicate rationally is proof of their intelligence.*

But why would it need to be theirs? They might share ours. Keeshah and Yayshah have as much a sense of individual identity as do Tarani and I—more, I corrected wryly, considering that the question of "Who are you?" is a multiple-choice test for Tarani and me.

"You say she would have known, in the Valley," I said to Tarani. "Do you mean she doesn't know, now?"

"I think she does know, at least in a general sense," Tarani said. "But she cannot tell me. She does not think in 'days' as we do. When I ask, she says only: 'soon.'"

I looked over at the silhouette of the sleeping female. As she rested on her side, the underslung swelling that held the cubs—she had told us there were three— mounded out, higher than the cat's hips, and rose and fell with Yayshah's breathing.

"We'll be in Thagorn in two days," I said. "The cubs won't arrive before then, will they?"

"If the birth were that close," Tarani assured me without hesitation, "she could not have left the Valley. For the last day or two, she will be too large and weak to move around much."

Tarani finished her berries and set aside the pack. I had been collecting my berry pits in one hand; now I threw them all away from me and watched them scatter into the ground cover. I leaned back against the boulder. Tarani joined me and rested her head against my shoulder. I put my arm around her and drew her close against my chest.

"I miss the feel of your body against my back when I ride," I said, my mouth brushing her dark headfur. "If Yayshah ever gets tired of you . . ."

She punched me in the side, and we wrestled playfully for a few seconds. She pulled free and knelt a few feet away, panting from the exertion, but laughing at me.

When her gaze fell on Yayshah, I felt a twinge of jealousy at the tenderness that appeared in her face. Only a twinge.

"I think it good that we are going no farther than Thagorn," Tarani said. "When I asked you if it would harm the cubs for me to ride her, as she wished, do you recall what you said?"

"That she's the best judge of that," I answered.

"She may not be," Tarani said seriously. "She is the first of her kind to bear cubs outside the Valley, and she can rely on instinct only to a limited extent. She will know when the cubs *are* endangered, of course, but I do not feel sure that she can prejudge what *will* endanger them. Do you see?"

"I see," I assured her. "But remember that in Thagorn, she will be in as natural an environment as we can provide for her—forested hills, free-running game, the company of other sha'um. Please don't worry, Tarani," I said, aware that I was repeating the same thing I had told Keeshah. "Yayshah will not suffer harm from any action of ours."

"I hope not, Rikardon. I—I couldn't bear it. Volitar died because of me, and Lonna—" Her voice choked off. I felt an odd sensation, like the crawl of an electric shock up my arm. Only this was *not* physical. It tingled in my mind. And it seemed to be getting stronger.

Is Tarani doing this? I wondered. *Or is somebody doing it to her?*

Whatever it was, it was most certainly affecting Tarani. She was kneeling in the viney ground cover. Her hands—long, finely boned, graceful—tensed on her thighs, and her whole body went rigid. She started making gasping sounds.

Yayshah twitched awake and looked at Tarani.

"Forgive me, Yayshah," the girl gasped. "I would control it—but I cannot—" *She's doing it herself*, I realized. *She's doing it to herself.*

"Tarani," I whispered, scrambling over the short distance between us to encircle her wire-tense body with my arms.

She struggled, pushing at me almost feebly, as though her hands had gone to sleep and she couldn't quite judge where they were. "Rikardon, please let me go," she moaned.

I held on to her squirming body with some difficulty. The fur on the back of my neck and on my hands stood on end. A charge was building inside Tarani, a kind of pure-thought energy that seemed to reach out to touch my mind, which recoiled as if it had been singed. Out of the corner of my eye, I saw Yayshah surge to her feet, her eyes wild, the fur around her neck rippling out.

"Get away," Tarani said, her voice muffled against my shoulder. Her efforts to free herself intensified. "Please, darling, move away, *get away from me I do not want to hurt you!*"

"No," I said—yelled, rather, for the sensation felt like a physical noise. "I won't let you go. Whatever this is, we'll beat it together."

In a sudden reversal, Tarani threw her arms around me and held on desperately. Her whole body was trembling; I could almost feel her fear in my fingertips. The shift in balance tipped us over. My shoulder struck the ground just as all hell broke loose.

Tarani screamed, and the sound was both expression

of and reaction to the searing raw emotion that burst forth from her. It was as though everything she had lived through in the past five years had been gathered together and distilled to the essence of experience, mixed liberally with Tarani's power of illusion, and broadcast in one giant feedback whine.

Fear joy guilt love loneliness disappointment shame frustration anger anxiety pride triumph love grief fury sadness satisfaction pride shame terror fury love guilt rage fear . . .

It was instantaneous.

It was devastating.

I blacked out.

Keeshah woke me, nuzzling my shoulder with a whiskered cheek, my mind with his anxious questions. My head hurt. Something . . . something had happened—but what?

All right? Rikardon? All right?

Uh-n-n . . . yes, Keeshah, I'm okay, I think.

I opened my eyes to see his head looming above me, the silver-flecked gray eyes fixed on me. I knew he wouldn't believe I was really okay until I touched him—but when I tried to lift my arm, I discovered that it was cramped and tense, clutching Tarani's still form.

Memory.

Panic.

I fought it down, freed one hand, touched her throat. I breathed again when I felt the slow, strong pulse beating there. I noticed, now, that she was breathing easily; I had been too startled and frightened to sense the significance of that rhythmic pressure against my chest.

I forced my stiff body to move, and rearranged Tarani until I had my other arm free. I laid her back into the vines gently, then went to get my water pouch and pour some of the lukewarm liquid into my headscarf. Like the rest of our clothing, it had seen better days, but the coarse linen soaked up the water thirstily. I returned to

18

Tarani and pressed the wet cloth to the girl's forehead, cheeks, and throat. My hands were still shaking.

Wake up, Tarani, I urged her silently. *Please, wake up.*

The girl's eyes popped open, and her body went tense as a bowstring.

"Easy," I said. "It's over. Take it easy, sweetheart."

The wildly staring eyes turned toward me and focused, and my heart jumped at the look of joy that swept into her face. She levered her upper body away from the ground and threw her arms around my neck.

"Thank God you aren't hurt, Ricardo!" she said.

In Italian.

A chill crept up my spine. I held her tightly for a moment, then I pulled gently at the girl's shoulders, separating us. The joy had been replaced with puzzlement and fear.

"Rikardon," Tarani said, clenching and unclenching her hands around my upper arms. "What happened?"

"Don't you know?" I asked her.

She looked at me in confusion, seemed about to speak, then turned her face away. She pulled a leaf from a vine and began shredding it with her beautiful hands.

"I only know I feel . . . peaceful."

I put my hand on her cheek and turned her face up to mine. For a moment, I searched that face for any sign that she knew she had just spoken to me in a language totally alien to her. But it was just the same as it had been on that first occasion in Eddarta.

Tarani had no idea what she had said.

What *Antonia* had said.

I avoided that thought and tried to answer Tarani's question. "You've been letting grief and sadness build up in you for a long time, Tarani. You haven't had a chance to let any of it go—you've been through too much, too quickly. What happened—well, you screamed, that's all. With your voice . . . and your mind."

"My mind . . ." she echoed, then panic wrenched

19

her away from my grasp. "Yayshah!" She jumped to her feet, looking around for the brindled gray cat. A rumbling from the spot between the boulders betrayed Yayshah's location, and Tarani ran headlong toward the dark female.

Yayshah crouched awkwardly, her tail lashing and her neckfur raised into a spiky mane. She backed away as Tarani approached her; pulling back her lips to expose the wide, sharp tusks at either side of a range of formidable teeth. Tarani faltered, stopped.

"Yayshah—please," Tarani pleaded, moving forward slowly and fighting to keep her voice steady. "Do not be afraid, it is over—"

I tensed, knowing it was foolish, that there would be nothing I could do if Yayshah attacked. It was only when the female calmed and Tarani placed her hands on the furred head that I felt myself relax.

Out of the corner of my eye, I saw Keeshah watching, seemingly unconcerned.

Did you know Yayshah wouldn't harm Tarani? I asked him.

Tell woman to leave, Keeshah said, not bothering to answer me. *Female must eat.*

Keeshah moved back up the hillside, and began dragging the carcass of a glith toward us. The glith were deer-sized animals that lived both wild and domesticated. Remembering our recent diet of dried foods and berries, I had an impulse to cook glith steaks for dinner. Looking at the bloody carcass, its throat torn clean away, changed my mind.

I started to call Tarani away from the female sha'um, but the girl was already walking toward me. "How odd," she said. "It was almost as though Yayshah did not recognize me."

Maybe she didn't, I thought. *Maybe she sensed that moment when you were Antonia, in the same way Keeshah knew Ricardo was different from Markasset, when I woke up in the desert.*

20

Tarani was watching me. "Did you hear me, Rikardon?" she asked. I nodded. "Have you no guess as to why Yayshah acted that way?"

"None," I lied, mentally shrugging my shoulders. "Remember, your experience with Yayshah is unique— very little of my understanding of Keeshah's behavior will be transferrable to Yayshah."

She was quiet for a moment. "There is something you are not saying," she said at last. Before I could frame an answer, she laughed and stretched. "Ah, but I feel too well, too *clean* to begrudge you your secrets, my love." She turned, whirled, twisted—danced across the rough hillside with all the grace and beauty I had seen in her when she had performed on stage. Even in her tattered desert tunic and trousers, wearing glith-hide boots that had been scarred and ripped by the pebbly slopes of the Well of Darkness, she was elegant, and I shared her joy in that physical expression of her mental release. Yet I couldn't share it completely.

Tarani doesn't even know she knocked me cold with that psychic blast. She took my word pretty easily for what happened—didn't ask questions, contradict, apologize. That's very unlike my articulate, outspoken, inquisitive Tarani.

She's blocking the memory of the outburst, I realized. *Little wonder; it must have been brutal for her. But she's also blocking that moment of total confusion while she was waking—the few seconds in which Antonia surfaced.*

That's three times, now, that Antonia has spoken clearly and directly to me—each time with words of love.

Why do I get the feeling that, in spite of all the complications, I'm a very lucky man?

21

3

Tarani was cheerful the next day and I decided, no matter how scary the experience had been for both of us, that I was glad she had found some expression for the emotions she had been repressing. Nothing was said between us about the incident; she seemed to forget it, and that suited me just fine.

It was on the afternoon of the following day that Keeshah woke me from a movement-lulled daze to announce: *Sha'um. Man.*

I sat up as we topped a rise and saw the sha'um and rider at the base of the hill. The animal stood halfway in a clearing, his hindquarters still hidden in high brush. His head and ears were up, and his nose pointed in our direction.

The Rider was sitting high behind the cat's shoulders, stretching as tall as he could, scanning the hillside. The wide-brimmed desert hat of the Sharith uniform effectively hid his face, but I recognized the pale marking that swept up one cheek of the sha'um. I remembered him as Borral, and that gave me the identity of the Rider.

"Raden!" I shouted. "Up here!"

The boy's head snapped up and he waved wildly. "Welcome, Captain!" he shouted back. "We have been waiting . . ."

Tarani and Yayshah came up beside me.

The boy's arm froze in mid-wave. His legs relaxed their normal tension against the sha'um's side, and dangled awkwardly; Borral moved slightly to balance the boy's shifting weight.

Tarani's look of weariness was replaced by one of delight, and she stroked the fur on the dark female's neck. "Come, Yayshah," she said. "It is time you began to meet our friends."

The boy's pose didn't change as Yayshah made her way, carefully and heavily, down the gentle slope of the hillside. I directed Keeshah to follow her, stirred by an amorphous uneasiness. That feeling didn't improve when I got close enough to Raden to see his face clearly in the shadow of his hat brim. The slack jaw and gaping look of surprise, I had expected. But his eyes were stretched wider than I would have thought possible, under his prominent supra-orbital ridge, and his gaze was fixed on the two females with what I can only describe as a look of sheer terror.

"Raden, is it?" Tarani asked. "I am Tarani, and this is—"

Tarani leaned forward to bring her left hand backward along the female's jaw. The boy interrupted her, his wild eyes turning to me.

"Captain, would you and—er—the lady Tarani mind—I mean—if you would care to rest here—I'll tell the others that you and—er—the lady Tarani have come back—that is, if you—"

"We'll wait for you here, Raden," I said.

"What?" Tarani demanded.

The boy glanced at her briefly, then looked at me with an unconscious pleading.

"Take word back to Thagorn, Raden," I said. "Say that Tarani and I—*and our sha'um*—request the shelter of the Sharith."

"Aye," was all he said, nodding vigorously while he

23

and his sha'um . . . "escaped" is the only word that really fits.

As soon as the boy was gone, I slid down from Keeshah's back—and was met by a frontal assault by Tarani.

"Did I hear the 'Captain' of the Sharith *ask* for shelter among people who owe him allegiance?"

Challenge sounded in her voice and emanated from the tense lines of her body as she faced me. I bristled, but caught my anger just in time. *She doesn't know what I went through in accepting that "allegiance,"* I reminded myself. *The doubts I felt, the responsibility I shouldered, the . . . totalness of feeling during the ceremony. It's not an "I say, you do" kind of situation; it's bigger than that. But I can't explain all that to her—not now, when her every thought and emotion is taken up with Yayshah's welfare.*

"You heard the Captain of the Sharith admit that there is no existing protocol for our present situation, and invite a committee discussion for establishing some."

"*Protocol?*" she echoed, then relaxed a little. She even smiled a little. "I think I see," she said. "The boy was startled by seeing a woman riding a female sha'um. You wish to give the others more warning. Is that not it?"

"Yes," I agreed, lying by implication and breathing a sigh of relief when Tarani accepted that answer and turned away.

In point of fact, she had pinpointed only part of the reason I had, on impulse, moved our "official" meeting with the Sharith away from the wall which contained and protected the valley which contained Thagorn. The rest of it would have been less comfortable to explain to Tarani.

It had taken seeing that boy's face to remind me that the entire body of Sharith had not ridden with us, desperate for our lives, back into the Valley of the Sha'um with Keeshah, that they had not witnessed,

24

participated in, agonized over Yayshah's choice to leave the Valley. Their understanding of the situation would be based, at first, on merely visual evidence—that a woman had brought a female out of the Valley, a *pregnant* female, at that.

I couldn't project what their reactions would be because, in spite of my title, I wasn't part of their tradition-centered society. Neither Ricardo Carillo of twentieth-century Earth nor Markasset of Raithskar could identify closely enough with the Sharith to have any insight as to whether their view of a woman rider would be respect or contempt, awe or outrage.

My only prior experience with their attitudes had occurred through Thymas, who had been willing to let the woman he loved be bounced and dragged in an uncomfortable cargo net, slung between two Riders, rather than consider the possibility of Tarani riding second on his sha'um. Yet there had come a time, after that, when Thymas would have invited Tarani to join him, if his sha'um had been capable of carrying double. Time—and exposure to the real Tarani—had been all it took to break him out of his attitudes.

That's really what I'm doing, I thought, *buying time. If there's going to be a confrontation, I want it out here, away from public view, where we'll have time to explain, negotiate, whatever it takes to make Thymas and Dharak see the real situation.*

It took only one look at Tarani to tell me that, far from my having deceived her with my "easy answer," she had simply not required any further explanation. If her silence and the grim set of her jaw weren't evidence enough that her logic had followed my thinking, Yayshah's restlessness would have expressed Tarani's mood.

The female settled down only to grumble to her feet and paw at the ground in another location, tearing new growth and scattering dead leaves and digging a shallow trench to accommodate the bulging curve of her belly. In contrast, Tarani stood dead still in the center of the clearing, her arms crossed, waiting.

Keeshah tried to help Yayshah with her bedmaking, and got a clawless swat across his nose for his trouble. He snarled and retreated and, for once wise, I followed him. I found a smooth-sided rock half-buried in the undergrowth at the edge of the clearing and used it as a backrest. Keeshah sprawled out beside me, stretching his neck to lay his head across my legs. I scratched behind the ear I could reach, and we drifted off into a communion of contentment.

Keeshah's head lifted suddenly, startling me awake— and making me aware that I had dozed off. The clearing looked the same, except that it was Yayshah who was still and Tarani who paced.

The female sha'um had dug and crawled her way into the thick underbrush; it wasn't until I caught the reflective glow of her eyes that I could look for and distinguish the silhouette of her body against the green-black of the shadows.

As I struggled to my feet, dusting off what passed for my clothes, Tarani stopped her pacing and looked southward, shading her eyes against the bright sky with her hand.

"Yayshah tells me another sha'um is approaching—but only one. Can it be the scout returning?"

"It could be," I said, "but it isn't. Keeshah recognizes the scent. It's Ronar."

Tarani snapped around to face me. "Thymas?" she asked. "Alone?"

"That's how it looks," I agreed, suddenly torn with indecision. *I shouldn't say this*, I thought, then said it anyway. "Would you—um, would you like to be alone when he arrives?"

She stared at me several heartbeats longer than I thought I could stand. Finally she sighed, and some of the tenseness seemed to drain out of her stiff shoulders. "If I were not so concerned about Yayshah," Tarani said, "that remark might have made me very angry—as yet it may, when I do have will and energy to spare. What will it take, my love, to put Thymas in your past as well as mine?"

I hoped I would have said something sensible in response to that, like an apology for being stupid and insensitive—but movement in the southerly brush drew our attention. A smallish, tan-colored sha'um stepped into the clearing, nearly carrying a smallish, good-looking young man.

I had no difficulty recognizing Thymas, for three reasons. First, even if I hadn't remembered Ronar myself, Keeshah's mindvoice acknowledged the other sha'um with wordless caution—the initial antagonism between Thymas and me had stimulated a lasting lack of trust between our sha'um.

Second, the twisted tip of a dakathrenil branch caught at the wide brim of the boy's uniform hat and dragged it back, revealing the startling pale headfur that provided such a handsome contrast to his brown-toned skin. The short, bristly-but-soft headfur of most Gandalarans started out anywhere from blondish to golden brown and darkened with age. The light color and extraordinary thickness of Thymas's headfur was a family trait; it made his appearance distinct.

Lastly, as the hat caught on the branch, the bead-tightened string that fastened under the chin dragged the boy backward, half off the back of the sha'um—and the snarl of frustration we heard from this Sharith marked him unmistakably as Thymas.

I tried to control a smile, but Tarani didn't bother. She laughed out loud.

"Hello, Thymas," she said.

The boy's body and voice stilled for a moment, then he let himself fall off the other side of the sha'um. He scrambled out through the space under the belly of the cat, who lifted one front paw and watched him curiously. He was hatless; he whooped with delight and came at us, catching each of us in a one-armed hug.

I was touched and startled by his uncontrolled display of gladness, and I returned his quick, hard-muscled hug with a surge of fondness for the boy.

Man, I corrected myself. *And while I'm at it, I'd best remember who he is—probably the next leader of the Sharith—and that we've fought and ridden together. It's not fair to him to define him only in terms of what he once was to Tarani. We had a rocky start, but he's my friend now, too.*

I felt slightly ashamed that I couldn't hold back the familiar afterthought, always present when I considered Thymas in action or motive: *I think*.

He let us go, saying: "It took you two long enough to get here. I have had our scouts riding triple distance, watching for you, ever since I got back. When you have rested, you must tell me . . ."

He seemed to really see us for the first time. His pleasure at our meeting had given his face an unaccustomed look of openness and youth. I watched it change, return to its normal intent seriousness as he absorbed the significance of Tarani's thinness and the tattered rags we were wearing.

"I should have stayed with you," he said at last. "What happened?"

It had never occurred to me to wonder what our fate might have been if Thymas *had* remained with us, and I paused now to let speculation sweep through me.

Ronar couldn't have carried the three of us, even had he been willing, I thought. *And I can't see that I'd have acted any differently with him there—I would still have been stubbornly, compulsively, insanely possessive of the Ra'ira. It's possible Thymas and Tarani, together, might have knocked me out and Thymas could have gotten away with the stone. It's also possible that Obilin and his dralda would have caught all of us, and the presence of a sha'um would have made the "cover" story I gave Indomel less acceptable, so that we would never have had the opportunity to escape again.*

Hindsight is next to useless, anyway, I sighed to myself. *Thymas, Tarani and I each did exactly and only what seemed right at the time. The boy doesn't need to feel any responsibility for something he couldn't control.*

While I was thinking all this out logically, Tarani reached out a hand to Thymas's shoulder and squeezed it. "You would only have put yourself into danger, as well—which would have gained nothing," she assured him softly. Her thumb traced the scar left on the boy's neck by the vineh who had attacked us on our way to Eddarta.

Thymas caught his breath at her touch, and grabbed her hand. "The wound had healed," he said bitterly. "I left you because—"

Because three's a crowd, I finished the thought for him. *Because you knew Tarani cared for me. In your place, loving her, not wanting to hurt her, knowing her affection had changed—I'd have been mighty uncomfortable.*

Tarani finished the thought aloud, with a less personal answer. "Because it was time for you to leave us," she said. "There is no purpose or value to restructuring the past, Thymas."

"What did happen?" he demanded. He dropped Tarani's hand, paced away from us and turned back, every muscle tense. "The Ra'ira?"

He was asking *me*, and I had to remind myself of Tarani's words in order to fend off the guilt that bounced up from a not-too-well-hidden corner of my mind. In spite of all my effort, the idea of admitting failure to Thymas made me feel like a truant schoolboy, and hard on the heels of guilt came resentment that the boy had such power over me.

I choked on that flood of emotion, and managed not to express any of it. Once more, Tarani answered in my place.

"Indomel has the Ra'ira," she said. "But he has had ill luck learning its use. It will be ours again soon."

"Soon?" Thymas gasped. "What does that mean, 'soon?' We went all the way across to Eddarta, we *had* it in our hands—*what happened?*"

"Do not speak to me in that tone," Tarani said. Quietly.

Thymas took a step backward.

"It will be easier on all of us," I said, "if we only have to tell this story once. Will the Lieutenant be joining us here, or shall we ride to Thagorn to meet him?"

Nobody missed the message hidden in those words: *You're second banana, boy. Take us to your leader.* Thymas bristled and turned to me, obviously more comfortable with the familiar challenge I represented.

"My father doesn't know you're here," Thymas said.

"But Raden—surely the scout reported—"

"To me," Thymas said. "It's the way things are done, now. And he made no sense, with his chatter. I decided to check it out for myself before I troubled Dharak."

I resisted asking how important information could "trouble" the Sharith leader. I also had some questions about "the way things are done, *now*" according to Thymas's interpretation, but I held them back. I even tried hard to sound civil.

"Then let's confirm Raden's 'chatter.' Tarani, would you like to introduce Thymas to our new friend?"

"Yayshah," Tarani called quietly.

The female sha'um had remained absolutely still since the entry of the strange sha'um into the clearing. Ronar had to have been aware of the female's scent, but he had, apparently, been too occupied with recognizing and keeping an eye on Keeshah to inform his rider of her presence.

Thymas jumped as the bushes behind me shook and the massive form of the darkly brindled female materialized from the shadows. Yayshah moved cautiously, her gracefulness only slightly impaired by her bulk, to stand between Tarani and me.

"Thymas, this is Yayshah," Tarani said, reaching up under the cat's throat to draw her hand along the left side of Yayshah's jaw. "As you can see, she carries cubs. She and I seek the shelter of Thagorn, so that her cubs may be born among their own kind."

"So it *is* true," Thymas breathed, staring with shining eyes at the female. "Raden will have my apology—as do you, Tarani, for . . . for my doubts," the boy said, with a slight but deferential from-the-waist bow. "May I greet Yayshah?"

"We will be honored," Tarani said.

Thymas stepped toward the female, his hand extended to touch her cheek.

Yayshah stood still, but her neckfur lifted.

Keeshah, still behind me, stepped closer, a soft warning vibrating from his throat.

An equally soft answer came from Ronar, who tensed and crept toward us from behind Thymas.

Thymas looked around at both the males, puzzlement clearly written on his face.

"Yayshah's cubs are also Keeshah's cubs," I said. "I've told Keeshah you mean his mate no harm." I was doing just that through my mindlink with the sha'um as I spoke to Thymas. "Keeshah left the Valley early; it will take some time for him and Yayshah to be comfortable with other people around."

"Yayshah is Keeshah's mate?" Thymas asked. I nodded. The boy sighed. "As I should have known," he said and, to my amazement, bowed to me in exactly the same manner in which he had bowed to Tarani. "It is still my wish to greet Yayshah. Will Keeshah permit it?"

If Tarani had been blessed with neckfur, I would have

been able to hear it snap to attention. For once, though, I was ahead of her—because my reaction to Thymas's question was identical to hers. "The choice is solely Yayshah's," I snapped.

"Yayshah will greet you willingly now," Tarani said, stroking the female's neck in a soothing gesture.

I could see by the look she threw me that Tarani was struggling to keep her thoughts calm. Thymas looked at me for confirmation of her permission; I became interested in a pebble beside my right boot. From the corner of my eye, I watched Thymas move in toward Yayshah, hesitate once as the female twitched her head into a slightly different position, and finally stroke the fur under her chin.

After a few seconds under Thymas's touch, the female's ears came forward and her eyes closed. Everybody relaxed. A little. Thymas stepped back finally, his face glowing with pleasure.

"Thagorn is honored that Yayshah has chosen to come here to shelter her cubs," Thymas said. "On behalf of the Sharith, I . . ."

"Only the Lieutenant may speak for the Sharith," I interrupted.

Thymas whirled on me, struggled for a moment against his anger, then gave up. "What you mean is, *I* have no right to speak for the Sharith," he snarled.

"I mean that, no matter what you say, we won't ride into Thagorn without Dharak's consent."

"Rikardon, can you think that Dharak would serve us differently than Thymas?" Tarani asked.

"No. I just want—"

"You just want to remind me that *you* are the leader of the Sharith, not I. Well, *Captain*, why bother Dharak at all with so small a matter as the first female sha'um who has ever left the Valley, and the first woman . . . Rider?"

The word shocked us all, coming from Thymas. Tarani came around Yayshah to take the boy's hands.

"I am not yet all that is implied by that honored title," she said. "But I am deeply moved that you can accept . . . what has happened for Yayshah and me."

"But there, you see, is the answer," Thymas said, smiling as he held Tarani's hands in his. "*You* have done this thing; therefore it must be right."

That kid's moods are as reliable as venetian blinds, I thought. *Snap—light. Snap again—dark. Smile at her, snarl at me.*

Just a minute, though, I reminded myself. *Wasn't I treated to an elegant bow of respect just a moment ago? But that wasn't the "Captain"—oh, no. That was the Rider of the mate of the one and only female sha'um ever to leave the Valley, with Tarani, who can do no wrong!*

I realized I was working myself into a four-star snit, and I stopped and took three deep breaths. The breathing helped. What didn't help was that Tarani and Thymas were still hands-on, eye to eye and nobody had noticed my extraordinary display of self-control.

What the hell's the matter with me? I wondered. *Isn't this what we wanted—for Tarani and Yayshah to be greeted and accepted as part of the Sharith?*

That's what I wanted from Dharak and the rest of the Sharith, I reminded myself. *But Thymas is different. There's a lot of emotional history tied up with Thymas. His relationship with Tarani has to be part of it, but there's more to it, I know. Maybe the rest of the Sharith didn't really count. Maybe what I wanted was for* Thymas *to accept Tarani because I am "his" Captain.*

I closed my eyes against the scene of closeness between Thymas and Tarani.

You idiot! I scolded myself. *You're going to make a real mess of things if you don't sort Tarani from Thymas—her love from his respect, his feelings for Tarani from his feelings for you, and your reaction to both.*

While you're at it, work on recognizing the Rikardon/ Tarani team as something different from the Keeshah/

Yayshah bonding. Because of the nature of the link between man—check that—Gandalaran and sha'um, the feelings of the four of us for one another are all intertwined. It would be easy, but dangerous as hell, to assume the Gandalaran emotional link is exactly parallel to the one between the sha'um. Yayshah and Keeshah are committed to one another in a natural, instinctual way. You and Tarani have chosen one another—"destiny" notwithstanding. As far as I can tell, "destiny" has brought us together to fight together—loving one another was our own idea.

Thymas turned to me again, his manner icily formal. "I will ride quickly back to Thagorn, tell Dharak about Yayshah, and relay your request. Please follow at your convenience."

"If Dharak denies our request?" I asked.

"I doubt," Thymas said, with a trace of sarcasm, "that he would send *me* to you with such a message."

"Dharak will not refuse us," Tarani said.

Thymas smiled at her. "No, he will not refuse you—at least," he added, with a sardonic nod to me, "it is my opinion that when you reach Thagorn, the Lieutenant himself will honor and welcome you—" There was just enough pause to be noticeable. "—both of you. Tarani. Captain."

Ronar, complying with the boy's mental request, moved closer to Thymas and crouched. His eyes never left Keeshah, and I could still feel my sha'um's wariness toward the other cat. Thymas mounted Ronar, who surged to his feet, whirled, and headed south through the broken brush that marked their entrance. They stopped long enough to allow Thymas to retrieve his hat from the stubborn branch and wave it at us in farewell.

Tarani was smiling in the direction Thymas and Ronar had gone. "Being a friend to Thymas can be very trying," she said. "But rewarding. There can be no one else as full of contradiction and surprise as he is; his company is never dull."

She had been stroking Yayshah absentmindedly. The cat became restless and stepped away. In following the sha'um's movement, Tarani caught sight of the look on my face, and laughed.

"Rikardon, why do you refuse to give me credit for objective perception of other people? It surprised you that I recognized Zefra's madness and it seems obvious that you expected me to accept Thymas's swiftly changing moods without irritation."

"I guess I tend to put other people—and their feelings—into categories," I said. "Thymas—well, my feelings about Thymas are pretty complicated."

"And you believe mine are not?" she asked.

"I believe you love him," I said. "A lot can be forgiven if you love someone."

"Forgiven, yes," Tarani agreed, coming toward me. "But not necessarily ignored."

She put her hands on my shoulders, and her face grew serious. "We were discussing this before Thymas came, I believe?"

"We were," I agreed. "I didn't have an answer for your question then, but I do now. Thymas will never be part of my 'past,' Tarani—or yours. He is part of us as we are now. I know that you still love him." She tensed, but I stopped her intended interruption by pulling her against me. "I also know that what you feel for him is different, less . . . special than what we share. I say I 'know' that—my mind believes it, but my feelings don't learn as fast."

She pressed against me, her arms around my neck, and we stood there for a moment. I was nearly overwhelmed with the knowledge of the value of what I held, the loss I would feel if she were never to touch me this way again. She seemed to be in the same sort of mood, for when she finally pushed at me gently, signaling me to let her stand back, I could feel a trembling in her arms.

"It moves me to hear you speak directly and honestly

of what you feel," she said. "It seems, at such times, that I can truly touch you, that a barrier I sometimes sense between us is missing. Now, while you are open to me, listen with your 'feelings,' Rikardon. The kind of future a man and a woman might expect, a home and children and just being together, cannot be ours until we have settled the matter of the Ra'ira. Indeed, for that reason, we may never see such a future. But remember that, even while we are busy with what we must do, even while other people and other things capture our attention and our time, the very center of me is unfailingly and lovingly bound to the very center of you. We are linked, as surely as you and Keeshah, or Yayshah and I— with the difference you defined a few days ago. You and I cannot communicate these feelings directly; we must depend on words, and words can lead to misunderstanding." She smiled.

She's remembering one of the many times in recent history that I opened my mouth and started chewing on my foot, I thought. *I wish I could forget a few of those.*

"I ask you, Rikardon, to speak to me as clearly as you can, and I promise the same to you."

"It's a deal," I said, moving the words around the lump in my throat. "And for starters, how about this? Speaking for Markasset and myself, we have known and loved many women, in this life and . . . and in my other life."

Hypocrite! I accused myself. *I'm still covering up the truth. Is this speaking "clearly?"*

I pushed the guilty voice aside, answering: *Yes, it is the clear truth as far as my feelings are concerned, and they are most important right now.*

"Tarani, we—I—have never known anyone, man or woman, whom I admire, respect, and cherish more than you."

She gasped, and I felt her shiver. "You have a gift for language, Rikardon, and you have seen that your words have power over me. What you have just said will always be my favorite truth, for it speaks what I feel for you, as well."

I held her again for a brief and tender moment.

"As you pointed out," I said, "we must tend to other tasks—like introducing Yayshah to the Sharith and her new home."

4

Good, Keeshah grunted, as he stepped out onto the wide, brush-free caravan road. *Easier.*

I echoed his sentiment. It had been bad enough breaking our own trail across the rocky slopes of the Morkadahl foothills, where brush and boulders presented equal obstacles. For the last half-mile or so, we had been moving further downslope, looking for the road we had just found. Without the occasional bare rock to keep the ground clear of ground cover, we had been breaking trail literally, crashing through tangles of brush and forcing our way past natural walls of vines, interlaced among the twists of curly trunked, wild dakathrenil trees.

We might have chosen merely to cross the higher slopes and enter Thagorn from the side, but nobody suggested it. The valley held rich, well-watered soil, and beyond the cultivated areas—meaning the higher slopes—the wild growth made the stuff we were moving through look like the Kapiral Desert. Tarani had made that trip once, on foot, and still carried faint scars on her hands to testify to the struggle it had been. For the sha'um, with their greater bulk, basic four-point balance and less efficient grasping capability, going that way would have been unrelenting misery.

Besides, we had made a point of requesting permission to enter Thagorn's valley, and that meant, by every tradition Ricardo or Markasset recognized, going in by the front door—in this case, the front *gate*. The caravan road came west, more or less, from the Refreshment House at Relenor and led south, more or less, right in front of Thagorn. From there it followed the Morkadahls around the southern tip of the range and headed north to Omergol, a crossroads city noted for the richly veined green marble its natives mined from the hillsides.

Many of the Gandalaran cities I had seen were surrounded by walls, but there was no other wall like Thagorn's. It was more like a dam than a wall, its upper edge stretching level across the narrow opening into a fertile, steep-sided valley. Its lower edge followed the shallow-dish contour of the ground. At the center of its hundred-foot span, the wall stood some thirty feet high, and a double gate filled half that height. The doors of the gate were made of thick layers of laminated wood and braced with bronze fittings, and they were usually closed.

As the sha'um topped the ridge that marked the edge of Thagorn's valley, I could tell that the gate stood wide open—not because I could see the doors, but because I could see the people who formed a double line along the road and through the entrance to Thagorn's protected valley. The Sharith formed the edges of those lines, but behind them thronged the women, children, and "cubs"—boys thirteen to sixteen who had sha'um and were in training as Riders.

The line of people ended halfway between us and the gate, and at its opening, waiting to greet us, stood Dharak and Thymas, the boy a step or two behind his father. There had been the murmuring sound common to a crowd of people waiting for something. The hillside had blocked it from us, but we heard it—for the merest instant—as we came over the top. A frantic whispering

39

sound reached us as all eyes turned in our direction—down from the throngs on the wall, up from the waiting people. There was a long moment of total silence, then a roar of noise rose from the throats of the Sharith.

Yayshah flinched back at the sound, ears flattening and neckfur lifting. Tarani was startled, too, and I recalled that she had not been present at my "installation" as Captain, when I had been honored in this way.

They were shouting my name. It had moved me then, and it touched me now. Equal parts of pride and humility straightened my shoulders as I pulled myself into a sitting position and urged Keeshah downslope at a slow and steady pace.

I realized that Yayshah and Tarani weren't with me, and I directed Keeshah to slow even further, to give them a chance to catch up with us. When they didn't come up alongside immediately, I became alarmed and glanced quickly back.

I've been thinking about Yayshah being accepted by the Sharith, I realized. *It never occurred to me to wonder whether it would work the other way around.*

My fears had been groundless, though; Yayshah was following with no more display of unrest than an occasional twitch of her ears. Her bulk added to the already impressive stateliness of a sha'um's gait. I felt, as I looked at her, the reverence common to men of Gandalara and of Ricardo's world, a sense of the mystery of maternity. Added to it was a purely Gandalaran awareness, awe of the cat and of what it meant to see her here, outside the Valley of the Sha'um.

I made a very slight hand signal to invite Tarani to ride beside me, but she shook her head and kept Yayshah a couple of yards behind Keeshah. We were nearing Dharak and Thymas, so I didn't have time to argue with her, but I felt disquieted as I turned to face the Sharith.

The third repetition of "Rikardon and Keeshah!" faded just as I stopped some five yards from the end of the reception line. Dharak took a step toward me, and it was only then that I realized there were no sha'um visible, except for Keeshah and Yayshah. I slid off Keeshah's back to meet the Lieutenant on foot. It didn't matter much—mounted or walking, a man *with* a sha'um had an emotional and physical advantage over a man *without* one—but it made me more comfortable to be eye-to-eye with the straight-backed old man.

"Welcome back, Captain," Dharak said, fairly glowing with pleasure and extending his hand in front of him. I shook it, touched by the sincerity of his welcome and his adoption of my greeting gesture over his own.

"You look well, Lieutenant. I'm glad to see your arm has healed."

He flexed his left elbow. "Shola has great skill at setting broken bones," he said, and laughed. "It comes from much practice."

He looked me up and down.

"Shola will be glad to ply her kitchen skills on you, my friend; you look in need of a good meal."

"I wouldn't mind several," I said, pulling at the shoulder of my ruined tunic, "*after* I've had several baths." Shola was, most certainly, in the crowd around us, but Dharak's speaking of her as if she were absent reminded me that, for the moment, the Lieutenant and the Captain were engaged in a formal ceremony of greeting. "But I am not alone, Dharak, and I may enjoy your hospitality only if it is also open to all those in my company."

"Thymas has already presented your request, Carillo."

A tremor in Dharak's left arm drew my attention to his hands; they were clenched into fists.

So it did bother the old man that Thymas kept the scout's report to himself! I thought.

"There is another that must be heard," Tarani said as she walked forward to stand, sha'umless, beside me. Dharak and I both turned to her in surprise—Dharak,

41

no doubt, because she had interrupted whatever he had rehearsed to say to us, and I because of the peculiar tone of her voice. After an instant's study, I identified it, with more astonishment, as timidity.

"Dharak, you were injured—and your Captain might have been killed—because of me. I ask your pardon for the role of deceit and betrayal I played on that day. I also ask that you do not allow feelings toward me to color your decision about the female sha'um who walks with me now. She is in desperate need of rest. Though I wish to be close to her during this critical period, we cannot truly be separated—and if you cannot, in conscience, admit me within your walls, I will be content to lodge elsewhere, if I know she is comfortable."

Dharak stared at Tarani for what seemed a long time— but perhaps my perception was colored by the fact that I was holding my breath. Finally, the Lieutenant held out his hands to Tarani and spoke with touching gentleness.

"Thymas has told us why that happened, Tarani, and I would gladly have traded this broken arm for the life of the man you were trying to protect. Not my life, perhaps," he added with a smile, "but a broken arm— certainly."

"You are kind," Tarani said, placing her hands in the old man's. "I wish I could forgive myself so easily."

"You are welcome among the Sharith, my dear, as is your companion." He glanced at me, hesitated, then faced Tarani squarely again. "May I greet her?"

Well, I thought, *at least Thymas and Dharak talk to each other. I'd swear that it was Dharak's first instinct to ask my permission to greet Yayshah, just as Thymas did. The boy had to have warned him against it.*

Tarani released Dharak's hands and took a small step backward. The gray-brown cat came forward slowly. Tarani reached up with her left hand to stroke the side of the sha'um's muzzle and said: "This is Yayshah."

Dharak let the cat examine his open hand until her

42

ears came forward, then rubbed behind her ear. I could almost feel waves of tenderness and awe from the watching crowd as Yayshah closed her eyes and twisted her head against his hand. After a moment, Dharak stepped back into position between the rows of Riders, and the crowd's mood became more crisp.

"Captain, the Sharith are honored that you pay us the courtesy of requesting what you might command. Again, welcome—Rikardon and Keeshah, Tarani and Yayshah."

A shout rose from the crowd—no words or names, just a joyful sound. I felt my throat tighten with the special joy and terror that a demonstration of the respect of the Sharith always brought to me. Beside me, Yayshah flinched slightly, but I saw Tarani's hand moving on her neck, calming the big cat.

When the roar had died down, Dharak spoke again. "We have one request, Captain. You will have noticed that our sha'um are not with us." I nodded. "I can speak for the Riders, my friend, but not for our sha'um. Until we can be sure that Yayshah is accepted among her own kind, we are asking our sha'um to remain on the far side of the river, except when their Riders call them for exercise or patrol. We ask, therefore, that Yayshah and Keeshah find their home on the nearer side of the river, at least temporarily."

Keeshah, they want you and Yayshah to stay on this side of the river for a while, away from the other sha'um. Do you have any objection to that?

Food there? he asked.

I tried to remember. The Sharith kept tame herds of glith for their own meat, but allowed a large herd to run wild on the slopes of their valley, to provide natural game for the sha'um. I knew that the tame herds were restricted to the farther side of the river, which was the main residence area for the Sharith, but I couldn't see the possibility, much less the value, of placing any restrictions on the wild herds.

43

I think so, Keeshah. If not, I'm sure Dharak will see to it that you have good hunting.

All right, Keeshah agreed.

The mental exchange took much less time than a vocal conversation would have consumed. It was barely a second after Dharak had made his request that I looked toward Tarani, who moved around Yayshah so that I could see her nod her head.

"The sha'um consent," I told the Lieutenant.

5

We walked into Thagorn between the lines of cheering people—Keeshah and I in the lead, followed by Yayshah and Tarani, then Dharak and Thymas. The boy had stood by mutely throughout the ceremony of greeting, and he disappeared into the crowd as soon as we stepped through the gate.

The crowd started to dissolve, the crisp lines behind us fragmenting into clumps of people who drifted through the gateway, smiled at us uncertainly and from a distance, edged around us, and set off for the bridge that led to the family dwellings across the river.

I felt a coldness creep in, where a moment ago there had been only the warmth of joy.

"Dharak—" I began, but when I turned around, Shola was standing beside her husband, her eyes on me.

"I, too, bid you welcome, Captain," she said, extending her hands. "Our home is open to you—to you both. If you'd care to come with me now—?"

"Thank you, Shola," I said. "We will see our sha'um settled, then accept your invitation with pleasure."

"Thank you, Shola," Tarani said. The Lieutenant's wife gave the girl a brief glance and nod, then walked away.

The moment of silence that followed Shola's rudeness was awkward. Finally, Tarani spoke, her voice clipped and tight to conceal the hurt I knew she felt.

45

"Perhaps it would be better if I—"

I interrupted her. "Tarani and I will avail ourselves of one of the vacant houses," I told Dharak, not trying to hide my anger. "Join us later, and we will talk."

"Please, Rikardon," Dharak said. His use of my name, rather than title, caught my attention, as did the whispered pleading in his voice. "We must talk later, in truth—but for now, I beg you, it is very important that you and Tarani share our home. Shola—I will speak to her. If you can be tolerant for only a little while, she will change, I promise you."

Promise? I thought. *Only a fool—or a desperate man—would promise the actions of another person.*

"Tarani?" I asked.

She shrugged. "I spoke the truth to Dharak; as long as Yayshah is comfortable, I care not where I rest. You may choose for both of us."

I nodded to Dharak. "We will join you shortly," I said, and led Keeshah from the roadway without looking back at the Lieutenant.

I was deeply disturbed.

That's what I get, I told myself, *for thinking simplistically, and identifying Thagorn as only a place of rest. It's a place of* people, *which means it's just as busy and complicated as any other city—more so, I'd say, with sha'um part of the citizenry.*

When Tarani and I arrived at the Lieutenant's home, which was the only single-residence building gateside of the river, it was Dharak who greeted us, showed us to our rooms and offered the use of his private bathhouse. He and I waved at Tarani as she passed the uncurtained door of my bedroom; she smiled and flipped the end of her towel at us.

"I'm ready to talk," I said. "Why was it so important that Tarani and I stay here? I stayed in the barracks on my last visit."

"At your own request," Dharak amended. "And only *before* you became Captain." He looked away from me,

46

walked to a chair and examined the lattice-wood construction of its back. "I have spoken to Shola—with what result, I confess I do not know. If you find her company intolerable, Rikardon, then she and I will move to a vacant house, and you and Tarani may have this one."

I wanted to tell him what I thought of that idea, but I held back. *Dharak's an intelligent man, a wise leader*, I thought, *but this residence thing—he tenses up and won't look me in the eye. Something's screwy here.*

"Answer my question, Dharak," I said.

Something in my voice made him stop his fidgeting. Standing with his hand on the chair back, still facing away from me, he sighed and spoke.

"You remember, of course, that when you were here last, I had the feeling that Thymas was achieving a place of leadership among the younger Riders?"

"I remember. You said you hoped the Sharith would be more united under the leadership of me as Captain. I suspected, at the time, that it was your main reason for pressing me to accept."

The old man faced me then, snapping around in what was almost an "attention" pose. "It was not!" he denied. He would have said more, but I waved him silent.

"I told you what I believed then," I said. "I no longer think so, in spite of the present situation."

"The present situation?" Dharak echoed.

I had begun to put some things together, and I didn't like the answers I was getting. I let my anger show.

"Yes, the present situation, in which you are using the Captain of the Sharith as a weapon in a power struggle against your son. Why else would it be so important that I stay here, even when it may mean discomfort for Tarani?" I wanted to ask, as well, why Shola was acting so coldly toward Tarani, but that seemed beside the point at the moment.

I watched Dharak's face display shock and guilt, then harden into determination.

"What I do is no worse than what Thymas has done.

47

Since his return he has used the—I will call it 'glamour'—of his association with you to win, ever more strongly, the loyalty of the young Riders. The division is growing, Rikardon. You are entirely correct; I thought your presence in my home might be taken as a confirmation of my place as leader. This is more than a personal conflict between father and son, Captain. You know that the scout brought Thymas news of your arrival, but I heard nothing of it until Thymas himself brought me your request—after first attempting to greet you 'officially' for the Sharith. He would have liked nothing better than to surprise us all by riding beside you and Tarani into Thagorn."

"Then you believe he kept the news from you deliberately?" I asked.

"I do," the old man affirmed. "He knew I would not embarrass us all by withholding my approval after he had invited you—Yayshah included—to stay with us."

"Did he have reason to fear your *dis*approval?"

At that, Dharak paused. "No," he answered at last, "not if he had taken the time to think it out logically. But our . . . conversations have not been graced with rationality lately." He slapped at the edge of the chair and muttered under his breath. "Rikardon, the boy opposes me at every turn."

"Purposely?" I asked.

"Yes!" Dharak nearly shouted, then added more calmly, "Or no. It does seem we have a natural bent toward looking at things differently. Purposeful or not, however, the result is that we seem always to be at opposite ends of any situation.

"In the matter of your arrival—he could not have doubted that you, personally, would be welcome. But as to Tarani and her sha'um . . . he might have felt I would disapprove solely because *he* wanted them to stay."

I shook my head and placed my hand on the Lieutenant's shoulder. "Could he have thought, my friend, that your actions might be more influenced by Shola's wishes than by his?"

Dharak gripped my forearm with his hand and chuckled. "How well you read people, Rikardon."

"Tarani once said something of the sort to me, with as little reason. Shola has hardly been hiding her bad feelings toward Tarani," I said.

"Not from Tarani, perhaps," Dharak said, "but from me—she will not discuss it at all. It amazes me, Rikardon. At the mention of Tarani's name, Shola turns into a salt block. In all the years I have known her, I have never had to deal with this . . . this silence before. Anger, yes. Fury on occasion. Quiet despair when we finally accepted that our other son would never return from the Valley of the Sha'um. But in those, we were together. She aimed her anger at me, she shared her grief with me. This—cold, isolated bitterness confounds me."

"How long has this been going on?" I asked him.

"Since you and Thymas left in pursuit of Tarani."

I left Dharak and walked to the unglassed window. The latticework shutters stood open to reveal a view of the river, on the opposite side of the house from the main road and bridge. I braced my arms on either side of the narrow window and stared out at the peaceful countryside. Some three hundred yards away, the valley floor rose steeply into brush-covered hillside. High on the irregular slope, I caught a glimpse of tan moving with startling speed, flashing in and out of sight as it passed behind hills and denser brush.

I reached out for Keeshah with my mind, and found him busy and joyful, concentrating on getting the glith he had just killed back to Yayshah. I didn't bother him, but the familiar touch comforted me in this home that had been open and warm once, but seemed so no longer.

"With your permission, Dharak," I said, "I'd like to try to talk to Shola about this."

"Do you know what the matter is?" he asked, his voice revealing a blend of consternation and delight.

"I have a couple of ideas," I admitted. "Mostly, though, I'd like to make it clear that if Tarani is not welcome here, I cannot accept your hospitality." I looked over my shoulder at the Lieutenant. "And I will not stand for your vacating this house, Dharak. No matter what you feel the effect will be on the Sharith as a group, Tarani and I will leave."

"I understand, Captain," he said, the tone of his voice convincing me that he did understand, but still wasn't very happy about the situation. "It would seem there could be more important duties for the Captain of the Sharith than to settle domestic quarrels."

"There will be," I said, realizing as the words came out that they were a promise I didn't understand, but one I believed.

"Destiny" again, I thought.

"The Ra'ira?" Dharak asked.

I heard footsteps coming down the hallway, and wondered if they meant Tarani was through with her bath. Swiftly then came an overwhelming need to wash off the grime on my own body. I turned, took Dharak by the shoulder, and walked him firmly to the door.

"I told Thymas that story would have to wait until we were all together, so Tarani and I would need to tell it only once," I said. "I'm telling you the same thing."

Tarani appeared in the bedroom doorway just as Dharak and I reached it. Tiny droplets of water clung to her dark headfur, creating silver highlights in her widow's peak.

Tarani flinched back, crinkling her nose. "Forgive me, Rikardon, but now that I am clean . . ."

"I know," I assured her, laughing. "I'm going."

"Until dinner, then," Dharak said. He nodded to Tarani, pressed my arm lightly, and disappeared around a bend in the hallway.

The Lieutenant's private bathhouse was functional and

elegant, very similar to the one I had used in Thanasset's back yard in Raithskar. The roof of the small structure was bordered with brownish tile and covered with wood to form a sun-warmed reservoir for water from the nearby river. Opening the fill valve on the tile conduit and cleaning grime from the drain filter were daily tasks for the "working" group of older children, though occasionally they were pre-empted as punishment duty for Riders.

Someone must scrub this tile every day, I thought, as I lowered my body into the tile-lined depression that formed a deep, narrow tub. *As I remember, Thanasset's tub was this well-kept, too—and he doesn't have a rotating duty roster to take care of such details. All he has is Milda.*

The thought of Markasset's father and aunt stirred memories and longing. They were good people, sincere and caring. They had accepted me as a stranger, and even when they had learned—I had told them the truth as soon as I had known for sure—that Markasset's identity was dead, they had accepted me as family.

I stirred the pleasantly warm water and slid further down to let it lap over my shoulders. The water's touch had awakened all the abrasions and muscle soreness I had been ignoring for the past several days, then it had begun to soothe them. I sighed and closed my eyes, homilies like "It's the simple comforts that mean the most" and "You never appreciate something until you have to do without it" wandering through my mind. I braced my body, slipped into a languid reverie, and relaxed—truly relaxed—for the first time since I had left Raithskar nearly eight weeks before.

The slight chill of the cooling water roused me. I applied soap and coarse washcloth to my skin, opened the drain, and stepped out. It was only then that I realized that I had failed to bring a robe or fresh tunic. I rubbed away most of the water, then wrapped the roughly woven towel around my middle. I left the bathhouse with my skin tingling and my feet bare; I carried my boots and the rags I had been wearing at arm's length.

The aroma of roasting meat greeted me, and I left the stone-laid path to go around the back of the house to the kitchen side. The ground was covered with grassy plants; the wide, soft blades cushioned the sound of my bare feet as I rounded the corner of the house.

A girl was tending the fire in the bottom section of the domed brick oven. She shoved the ceramic door back into place and turned toward the house at about the same moment that I became part of the view. She shrieked, whirled to run, stopped to look, blushed furiously, and started to giggle.

I tried not to laugh with her—even a bare-assed Captain needs dignity. Lucky for me, Shola had heard the commotion and now she hurried out the door, drying her hands on her apron. She did a fair job of hiding her own amusement as she scolded the girl.

"Yena, where are your manners?" Shola said. She took the boots from my hand and held them out to the girl. "Take these down to the river and freshen them—mind you shake off all the dust before you touch them with water. Go on, now."

The girl took the boots, looked me over one more time, then fled, still giggling. Shola reached out for my clothes, then seemed to think better of it. "If you will put those on the ground beside the house, Captain," she said, rubbing her hands on her apron as if she had actually touched them, "I'll see to it Yena burns them—*after* dinner."

I tossed down the clothes and unconsciously mimicked Shola's gesture, rubbing my hands on the towel—which came loose. I grabbed at it in panic and replaced it before it slipped too far. I discovered I needn't have worried; Shola was looking at the heap of shredded cloth.

"Your clothes speak of suffering, Captain." She looked

up into my face, her own expression soft and caring. "They make me grateful to have you with us again."

"Thank you," I said. "You make me feel welcome, in every way but one."

Her face closed down and turned away. "If there is anything you need, Captain—" she said, her voice formal. I touched her arm.

"I think you know what I need, Shola."

Come on, Shola, I urged her silently. *Talk to me. Don't shut me out.*

For a moment I was afraid she was going to do exactly that, and I was poised on the edge of disappointment. Then she took a deep breath and announced to the wall of the house: "I am not the sort, Captain, who can pretend what she does not feel."

"Then why not say what you *do* feel?" I asked her.

She looked at me then, her eyes flashing. "There is no place in the Lieutenant's home for rudeness."

"You have made a place for it," I said, more sharply than I had intended.

"Have I not been polite to her?" Shola demanded.

"A cold and insincere gift that speaks your disapproval more clearly than words," I said. "You're deliberately trying to hurt Tarani. I want to know why."

"This is a personal matter between us, Captain— hardly worth your attention."

"I see," I said, meaning that I could see how this attitude was frustrating Dharak. "Tarani and I will be moving across the river after dinner, Shola."

"What? But . . . you cannot do that, Captain!" she said, stepping between me and the kitchen door as I moved toward it.

"Of course I can," I said. "As I recall, there are a number of vacant homes; we will not inconvenience anyone."

"I do not mean that," Shola said.

"What else could you mean?" I asked. Her lips tightened as my point got through to her. "Could you mean," I asked more gently, "that some actions say more than one thing to the people who see them? That our moving out of the Lieutenant's house could be seen by the rest of the Sharith as what it is—a reaction against your negative feelings toward Tarani—or as what it isn't—a withdrawal of support for the Lieutenant?"

"Please, Captain, it is bad enough between Dharak and his son; would you make it worse?"

"I would make Tarani comfortable," I replied.

"Is *she* more important to you than the good will of the Lieutenant of the Sharith?" Shola demanded.

"I have no fear of losing Dharak's good will—or Thymas's, for that matter," I said. "But the answer to your question is—yes."

Shola gasped. "That woman—will her evil never be done?" she raged.

"Evil?" I repeated, shocked.

"What would you call it, Captain, to seduce a boy for the sole purpose of murdering his father? To reach for power in every possible way—leaving the boy for his commander, coming between father and son so that neither might challenge the one she has chosen, going so far as to bring a sha'um mother to a strange place for the sake of winning respect she does not deserve!"

I flinched back from the tirade. I was glad that I had finally provoked a response from Shola, but slightly overwhelmed at its vehemence.

"What has Thymas told you," I asked, "of what happened when we left Thagorn?"

"Nothing," Shola said, obviously surprised by the apparent non sequitur. "He has said nothing, except that you obtained what you sought, and that Gharlas is dead."

I nodded. It fit.

I straightened my shoulders and looked down at the Lieutenant's wife. "I won't tell you you're wrong about Tarani, Shola. My saying it won't change your mind. But ask yourself how much of your anger toward Tarani is

54

based in fact—incidentally, you don't *have* all the facts—
and how much in fear."

"Fear?" Shola said. "Surely you cannot believe I
would fear a woman like that!"

"Fear of your family breaking up," I said. "Isn't it
easier to blame Tarani for driving Dharak and Thymas
apart than to admit that neither of them is perfect, and
that they're creating their own problems?"

I moved around her and stepped up to the kitchen
door.

"Do you still intend to leave?" she asked.

"Not tonight," I said, looking over my shoulder at her.
She seemed smaller, somehow, uncertain. *Maybe I got
through to her*, I thought. "If our leaving were to disrupt
the leadership of the Sharith, right now you'd blame that
on Tarani, too. You've had a long time to build up your
anger—the least we can do is give you a day or two to
really get to know Tarani. I only ask that you keep an
open mind, and see her as herself, independent of me or
Dharak or Thymas. Will you do that for me, Shola?"

She hesitated. "I will . . . try, Captain. I can promise no more than that."

6

I was still thinking of Shola as I turned down the hallway that led to the two guest rooms. I paused at my doorway, then continued on to stop before the tapestry hanging that provided private entry to Tarani's room. I had my hand up to knock on the flat stone sill when I heard a man's voice from inside the room. The words were softly spoken and indistinguishable from one another, but I recognized the voice.

I lowered my hand and went back to my room.

I was sitting on the edge of the pallet-lined ledge that served as a bed when Tarani knocked at *my* door half an hour later. I was dressed in a fresh "uniform"—tan trousers and tunic, with darker leather belt and boots (baldric and sword omitted)—and my hands were clenched together between my knees. The knock was so soft that I wasn't sure I had heard anything until Tarani pushed aside the door hanging and looked into the room.

"Rikardon? Why did you not answer? Why are you sitting here in the dark?"

"Dark?" I echoed, then realized I could hardly see Tarani as she walked across the room. As she passed in front of me, I heard a silky, whispering sound.

Tarani threw open the latticed shutters. The light that entered was already touched with evening dimness, but it brought Tarani into clear focus. She was wearing a long

56

gown of a pale golden color. The fabric was soft and sheer, and shimmered when she moved. It was simply cut to drape softly at the neckline and fall in a clean, straight line to brush the floor, and it had full sleeves that tied at her wrists. The shape of the dress accented her unusual height; its color complemented the paleness of her complexion and made the darkness of her headfur more striking; the effect of the outfit was to accentuate her regal bearing. Tarani looked like a queen.

She came toward me, smiling. "The dress is a gift from Thymas," she said. "He traded for the fabric, and asked Jori to make it for me. He called it a replacement for my dancing gown, but it seems much more elegant to me. Do you like it?"

I stood up to meet her, and took her hands. "You look magnificent in it, Tarani. Who is Jori?"

"Thymas's sister, the one who married Solenin. Have you not met her?"

"No, though I do recall the name, now."

"She is a good person, dotingly fond of Thymas, and I am grateful to her." Tarani's voice turned flat. "Shola, too, gave me a gown to wear this evening."

When she didn't go on, I said: "One of Shola's gowns would be too large and too short for you."

"Her gown is an ill fit in more ways than one, Rikardon. It was a bitter and grudging gift."

"When did she give it to you?" I asked.

"She met me on my way to the bathhouse and told me she would leave it in my room," Tarani said. She squeezed my hands. "Rikardon, even in this gown, I do not anticipate this evening with pleasure."

"I understand how you feel, Tarani," I said. "I want to ask a favor of you."

"A favor?" she said, frowning slightly. "Of what sort?"

"Silence," I answered. "When it comes time, this evening, to talk of Eddarta and Gharlas and Yayshah, I want to be the one to tell the story, and I'd like your permission to use my own judgment as to how much to tell."

She lowered her eyes. "Tarn's cellar?"

"Maybe," I said. "Who you are. What the Ra'ira is. Our plans. I may not tell all of it, but I want to feel free to make that choice without fear of surprising or hurting you."

"I am grateful for your consideration," she said, looking up at me again. Even with the light behind her, there was a glow in her dark eyes. She smiled. "I would like to say you need not have asked, but I fear you know me too well. You have my promise; I shall not interrupt you. You do not require my consent to reveal any matter relating to the Ra'ira; that is your choice, as leader of the Sharith. I give you the permission you ask, to share your personal knowledge of me."

"Thank you," I said, feeling humbled by her trust—and guilty, as usual. "Aren't you going to ask me why?"

She laughed and put her hands on my shoulders. "It would spoil my evening," she said. "I am so intrigued, now, that I am actually looking forward to the dinner I dreaded only moments ago."

I put my hands on her waist and pulled her a little closer to me. "There's something else I need to tell you," I said. She only tilted her head. "The reason it was dark in here when you came in—I knew Thymas was in your room. I closed the shutters to avoid eavesdropping."

"Why do you tell me this now?" she asked.

"Because of my promise—to be honest with you whenever possible. I came in here arguing with myself and fighting jealousy. I reminded myself that the last time I jumped to a conclusion—when I saw you kiss Thymas goodbye in Stomestad—I landed flat on my face."

She laced her fingers together behind my neck. "Would you have told me this," she asked, "if I had not mentioned Thymas? After all, this fine dress *might* have been Shola's."

"I would have told you anyway," I assured her. "I can't seem to help feeling jealous of Thymas and suspicious of his motives whenever he's around you. I want you to know that I have those feelings—and that I *am* learning to control them. This time, I didn't jump to any conclusions."

"Oh, but you did," she said, smiling. "You assumed he was inside my room, did you not?" I nodded. "He came to my *window*."

It was a small point, since Tarani's window was like mine—knee-low and ceiling-high, and plenty wide enough for Thymas to *step* through, had he wished. But in Gandalara, as in the world Ricardo had known, there are different degrees of privacy. A man and a woman talking together in full view of any passerby—whether or not anyone was, at that particular moment, passing by— was less suggestive of intimacy than that same couple holding their conversation enclosed within the walls of a room.

It made enough difference to me that I blurted out an admission that I had checked for the more welcome possibility. "But—when I closed my shutters, I didn't see . . . Oh."

"I see you remember that my room is at the corner of the house, and has *two* windows. And there is another item of information you do not have," she said. "The gift of the dress was second priority for Thymas. He told me that he had come to talk with you, but that you were not in your room."

"To me? Did he say what he wanted to talk about?"

"No. And I did offer to bring you a message. He is . . . different, Rikardon. There is a sadness in him, and little of the easy friendship we once shared. He seemed uncomfortable while we talked." She sighed. "Has Thagorn changed so much, Captain, or is it we who have changed?"

"The *world* is changing, remember?" I said. "Otherwise, would there be a female sha'um in Thagorn? How is Yayshah, by the way?"

"Rather cranky, I fear. Her mind is seeking a lair that her instincts will accept, but so far she has not achieved that compromise. The terrain in Thagorn is very different from what she knew in the Valley. And, unlike Keeshah, the Valley is all she has known. She will settle down in time."

"The cubs? Do you have any closer idea of when they are due?"

She shook her head. "There is no pain, only a heaviness that grows, day by day. I cannot say." She pulled me close and put her head on my shoulder. "It is not only Yayshah's relief I feel in being here, Rikardon. I am weary of traveling. I welcome the chance merely to be still for a time. I could wish for only one thing more— that we be accepted as friends here, and not—"

She broke off and pulled back suddenly.

"That is the difference I sensed in Thymas," she said, her eyes sad. "Distance. Almost a shyness. Courtesy with an undertone of fear, not at all the simple respect of one person for another."

"The respect of a follower for a leader," I said gently.

"Because he thinks of me, now, as yours? The Captain's woman?"

I almost laughed, but I could see Tarani was hurting. I had learned this lesson weeks ago, when I had swung violently between my commitment to become Captain and a deep need to be only one of the group. The look on her face brought back that pain.

"Because Yayshah came with you from the Valley," I said. "It's only here, among the Sharith, that the enormity of that simple act can be truly appreciated."

"But that is not an achievement, in the sense of planning and accomplishing a difficult task," she protested. "It—it merely *happened.*"

The way, I thought, *that it "merely happened" that Ricardo Carillo woke up in Markasset's body.*

60

Tarani's arms tensed against my shoulders. "Among the Lords of Eddarta, I should welcome this . . . acknowledgement of difference. There, only power commands respect, and only fear assures obedience. Among the Sharith, people whom I respect and care for as friends, this distance is disturbing, Rikardon. I am—it frightens me."

"Good," I said.

"Excuse me?" she said.

"I said, 'good,'" I answered. "You understand that when people treat you that way—sincerely, not out of fear as might be the case in Eddarta—it means they believe that you are wiser or stronger or more capable of being right than they are. *Because* you care for them, you don't want their trust in you to hurt them. If that responsibility didn't scare you, I'd be worried."

A frown crossed her face. "I hear contradiction in your words, Rikardon. First you say that it is not my association with you that brings me this special respect, and then you speak as though I have some role as leader among the Sharith. I do not."

"Not yet," I amended. "Because you're a Rider, you have a place in Thagorn. Because you're a woman, the *first* woman Rider, nobody's sure what that place should be." I smiled at her. "Don't be too concerned, darling. One thing we'll do this evening is make it clear that you're only a guest here, on your way to Eddarta."

"Perhaps that is why Shola seems so hostile toward me—she fears I will take her place of authority over the women in Thagorn. If that is so, then I need only assure her—"

"You need only let me do the talking, as you promised," I reminded her.

Her eyes glowed as she looked up at me. "This is part of the reason you asked my silence, is it not? To spare me the burden of confronting Shola to regain her friendship?"

"It is *part* of the reason," I admitted. "Not the only one. It must be nearly time for dinner," I said, and realized that I was getting anxious to have this done. "Shall we go?"

"In a moment," she said. My anxiety faded as her arms slipped around my neck and her face tilted up to meet mine.

Dharak and Shola were waiting in the dining room, already seated. Dharak stood up and came to the door to greet us when we arrived, his pleasure genuine, his admiration for Tarani obvious—to us and to Shola.

Dharak's wife was dressed in a tan sleeveless gown embroidered with gold thread at hem and neck. Jewels glittered at her wrists and throat. I surmised, from the quick flash of hurt in Tarani's face, that the gown Shola had given her would have compared badly against Shola's elegance.

Tarani said nothing to Shola, but turned to Thymas, who was arriving right behind us, to thank him again for his gift.

Dharak looked at Thymas suspiciously.

Shola glared at Tarani.

Thymas, whose capacity for subtlety seemed to be expanding, acknowledged Tarani's thanks with a smile, then announced: "Dinner smells wonderful."

I sighed and pressed the boy's shoulder as he passed me.

It is always hot in Gandalara, but it was frosty around the dinner table that night. The meal was delicious: strips of well-roasted glith served with savory vegetables, a richly grained bread with a creamy spread, and spiced fruit for dessert. It had Shola's expert touch, to be sure, but it was served by Yena and two other girls, who looked mainly at the dishes they carried, with an occasional sidelong glance at Tarani.

Conversation was little more than sincere compliments to Shola on the quality of the meal, to which she responded with a smile and a nod. It seemed to me she was trying to imitate Tarani's regal and composed manner, with little success. It was clear that, even had she worn the plainer, ill-fitting gown, Tarani would have outclassed Shola, and both of them knew it. Tarani proved it by being gracious but aloof, betraying none of her feelings. Shola proved it by projecting an air of resentment and defeat.

Dharak and Thymas, at opposite ends of the largish table, sat with their shoulders hunched, their neck muscles tense, and said very little. They might have been sensing the undercurrents across the table—I was sitting at Dharak's right with Tarani beside me and Shola across from me—and deliberately staying clear of them. They might have been caught up in their own tide of competition.

One thing's sure, I thought. *This meal is being wasted on this group. I'll be very surprised if we don't all get indigestion later.*

The meal finally ended, and the girls began clearing away the dessert dishes. It was the host's place to suggest an after-dinner drink at this point, and it had been Shola's habit to excuse herself from what was usually the "business end" of an evening such as this. I had thought that Tarani's presence might change things, but Shola stood up to help the girls—whether out of habit or in eagerness to escape the tension in the room, I couldn't say. I stood up with her, and she stopped in surprise.

"Please stay, Shola," I said. "I have promised a full accounting of what has happened since I left Thagorn. I know Dharak would share it with you, later, but I prefer that you hear it from me."

She stared at me for a moment, then dropped her eyes. "As you wish, Captain," she said.

Dharak cleared his throat. "Perhaps, Captain, we would be more comfortable in the sitting room? Would you care for some barut?"

"Later, perhaps, Lieutenant. For now, I feel the need of a clear head."

I walked around the table and offered Shola my arm. She took it with an air of surprise. Out of the corner of my eye, I saw Thymas extend his hand to Tarani, who smiled, shook her head, and followed us on her own.

Good for you, I thought.

7

When the others had found places in the large room—
Tarani on a padded ledge, Shola and Dharak in free-
standing chairs, Thymas on a fluffy rug in the corner—I
found myself wondering how to start what I had to say.

I'm the Captain, I reminded myself. *If I want these
people to communicate clearly, I guess I need to set an
example.*

"The Ra'ira is more than it seems," I said.

Thymas's whole body jerked in surprise, and I turned
to him.

"There will be no secrets among the people in this
room, Thymas," I said. "And there will be only honest
answers to any question I may ask. Is that understood?"

I looked around the room, and everyone nodded.
Dharak looked grim, Shola a little frightened, Thymas
angry but resigned. Tarani alone was totally composed,
because she had expected something like this.

"Thymas, I know that you have told the Sharith very
little about our time together—only enough to clear
Tarani of blame, and assure them that our purpose was
accomplished. I believe you kept silent because you felt
the story—and the decision of how much to tell—was
mine to make. Is that true?"

"Yes," Thymas said.

"I also think you kept silent because to tell the entire

story would have been to reveal what you believe to be your own failure and disgrace. Is *that* true?"

Thymas moved, crossing his legs, sitting up straighter, finally looking right at me. "Yes, I was ashamed to tell—"

"We'll get to that," I interrupted. "Since you came back, you've been trying to make up for that failure, haven't you, by relieving your father of some of his tremendous responsibilities, by trying extra hard to be a leader?"

Thymas only nodded. I whirled around to face Dharak, who was leaning forward in his chair.

"This seems to surprise you, Dharak. What did you think your son was doing, trying to take command of the Sharith from you?"

"No," the Lieutenant exclaimed. "That is—not really . . ."

"Not really?" I echoed, raising my eyebrows.

"Well, *yes*," he blurted out—to his credit, less angry than confused. "We disagree frequently, and many of the Riders side with him. I *have* been afraid of a division among the Sharith and—yes, I thought Thymas wanted such a thing."

Thymas made a wordless sound and rose up to his knees, but I didn't give him a chance to say anything.

"If it came to a choice between you and Thymas, who do you think the Sharith would choose?" I asked Dharak.

"Captain!" Shola said. I ignored her.

"Dharak? Answer. Do you believe they would choose Thymas over you?"

"Yes!" the white-haired old man shouted. "Why would they not? He is young, dedicated, strong—"

"Everything you're not?" I prompted. "He knows what he wants, while you're confused, is that it? When we talked about my becoming Captain, you as much as admitted that you see change coming but can't predict or control it, and it scares you. And you think Thymas is younger, more adaptable, more sure of himself. Look at what happened the night Tarani danced—you got yourself hurt, and *Thymas* killed the man who hurt you. That's proof, isn't it, that he's the better man? Isn't that true?"

"No!" Thymas shouted.

"Let him answer!" I snapped.

Dharak lowered his gaze. "It is all true," he said, rubbing his hands together. "It is all true."

"Captain," Shola said. I turned around; she was standing up. "You cannot keep me silent, Rikardon. You have shamed a fine man in front of his son—I thought no one could be so cruel."

"Did you think you had exclusive rights to cruelty?" I asked. She gasped. "What else would you call the games you've played with Tarani—doing everything you can to make her feel inferior and unwelcome, while meeting the 'letter' of courtesy?"

"I would call it the treatment she deserves!" Shola fired back.

"Why?" I demanded.

"She never loved my son! She tried to kill my husband! Her deceit and treachery have driven them apart. I have no cause to treat her with honor!"

"Not even if doing so would heal the break between Dharak and Thymas?" I asked.

She looked surprised, then her lips thinned. "It would not help."

"You're right," I said. "It wouldn't help, because Tarani didn't cause this separation in the first place. Dharak did it, because he failed as a leader."

"He is a fine leader!" Shola cried.

"Then it is Thymas's fault, because he has been sneaking responsibility away from his father."

"He has only tried to help!" Shola protested.

"Then it's *your* fault, Shola. If you had been more perceptive, more caring, quicker to act, you could have kept your family together."

It was very quiet in the room for about half a second, while Shola stared at me, caught up in horror and guilt.

Then it erupted in noise. Dharak and Thymas were on their feet, shouting at me; Shola was screaming accusations at Tarani, who was still sitting, but visibly shaken by what had just transpired.

"Quiet!" I shouted. "I said QUIET!"

Voices trailed off into silence.

"Sit down," I said. I realized I spoke sharply, so I added, more gently: "Please, everyone, sit down."

When they were all settled again—I wouldn't describe any of them as relaxed—I said: "Have you noticed that you're all glaring at *me* now, instead of one another?"

Thymas, for whom glaring at me was far from a new experience, spoke up. "Make your point, Captain—if you have one."

I sighed and looked around the room. All four of them looked exceedingly uncomfortable, only Tarani retaining some composure because she hadn't verbalized her feelings.

"I had hoped you would see the point without explanations," I said, and waited.

It was Dharak who broke the silence this time. "I see that each of us accepted blame for ourselves, but defended the others. Are you trying to teach us that we care for one another?"

"That's part of what I'm trying to say," I agreed. "You all *know* that, of course—but how often have you and Thymas mentioned it to one another lately?"

Neither Dharak nor Thymas, who sat across the room from his father, would meet my eyes.

"I noticed," Shola said, "that the lady Tarani said nothing in *anyone's* defense."

"I have to admit to being a little unfair, Shola," I said. "Tarani had some warning about all this. She didn't know what I would do, but she did promise to keep out of it. What do you suppose she was feeling, while you were accusing her of destroying your family?"

Shola started to say something, then merely shook her head.

68

"Tarani," I said. "How did you feel?"

"I was afraid," Tarani said, her voice pitched low but clearly audible. "I was desperately afraid that she was right. Certainly, your suggestion that Shola accept responsibility for Dharak's stubbornness and Thymas's self-doubt was preposterous. If their trouble began with Dharak's wound, then I am indeed at fault."

Shola was staring at Tarani, who was looking at her hands, lightly clasped in the lap of her golden gown.

"You won the match, Shola," I said, beginning to be very uncomfortable in my role as devil's advocate. "She admits it. Doesn't that make you happy?"

"Yes—no. Captain," she said, the tightness of the skin around her eyes speaking her distress, "I recall what you said this afternoon, that I might be blaming Tarani rather than Dharak or Thymas. I feel your point is that I am the one who caused the break between father and son and, rather than face so bitter a truth, I have placed Tarani at fault. Am I—can I be such a coward?"

Dharak rose from his seat, starting to speak, but I put my hand on his shoulder and walked past him to kneel in front of Shola. The pain and fear in her face were terrible to see. I took her hand and pressed my cheek against it.

"Is it cowardly," I asked gently, "to love Dharak and Thymas so much that you want them to be happy?" She shook her head, her eyes on our joined hands. "Of course not. The question is, can *you* make them happy? If they persist in being argumentative and misunderstanding each other, is *that* your fault?"

Shola's shoulders began to tremble. Gandalarans are physically unable to weep emotional tears—part of the water conservation system in their bodies—but they display sadness in a very human fashion. A choked, whimpering sound came from Shola's throat as she started to sob.

"Rikardon, in Zanek's name . . ."

Dharak pulled me away and put his arms around his wife. Shola leaned sideways in her chair to press her face against the Lieutenant's chest. Dharak stroked the light brown headfur and made comforting sounds.

Thymas grabbed my arm and turned me toward him.

"The point, Captain," he demanded. "Now."

I felt a more gentle hand on my shoulder, and looked around to see Tarani standing beside me.

"I know I promised not to speak unless asked, Rikardon, but I believe you are making your point to me, as well?"

I put my hand over hers and smiled at her. Shola's burst of emotion had passed, and she and Dharak, still clinging lightly together, watched Tarani expectantly.

"I believe Rikardon has tried to show us that we cannot forgive ourselves for mistakes which are totally understandable in others, and that we attribute the failure or unhappiness of those we care about to our own mistakes."

"And that we are, each of us," I added, "always ready to believe *we* have failed." I faced Thymas directly. "You still think we would have caught Gharlas in Dyskornis if it hadn't been for you and Ronar, don't you?"

The boy nodded, the muscles along his jaw tensing and relaxing.

"So, in order to avoid telling your father about your imagined failure, you don't tell him anything at all—a silence which he interprets as deliberate and antagonistic. He trusts and admires you, so he assumes you have a good reason for not trusting him—therefore, he has failed in some way. Meanwhile, Shola watches her family falling apart and figures it's her fault." I paced across the room, my voice rising with real anger and impatience. "All you have to do, for pity's sake, is *talk* to each other."

I stopped in the corner of the room, picked up a ceramic figure of a sha'um and turned it in my hands, not even looking at it. "You may wonder how I know so much about this," I said. "I'm good at recognizing self-imposed guilt because I came face to face with my own in Eddarta." I put the figurine down and looked at the others. Dharak, Tarani and Thymas were standing, and Shola was still seated, leaning against Dharak. They all watched me expectantly. I walked toward them, extending my hand. Tarani met me and took my hand.

"I promised I would tell you what happened after Thymas and I left Thagorn, looking for Tarani. I want you all to know—especially you, Shola—that some of that story is very personal for Tarani, and that she has given me her permission to share it."

Tarani came into my arms briefly, then turned aside and found a seat. Thymas and Dharak took the cue and sat down again.

"I learned all this in bits and pieces, but I wouldn't want to try to tell it the same way, even if I could reconstruct it for you. The story really starts more than a year before Tarani was born. . . ."

"So that's how it stands now," I said. "After Yayshah has delivered her cubs, the next step is to find Kä and the other sword. Any ideas?"

It was nearly midnight. My voice had roughened after the hours of talking, and I felt totally wrung out. The others had listened more or less quietly. Thymas had said a word or two of sincere sympathy to Tarani when I had described Lonna's sudden death at the hands of Obilin. There had been tension in the room at the beginning of the story, but it was gone now. Everyone's physical attitude betrayed a relaxed fatigue. Dharak and Shola held hands in the space between their armchairs. Thymas sat cross-legged on the floor. Tarani was half-reclining on the stone ledge underneath the windows. I was sprawled in an armchair.

"Dharak," I said, when no one responded, "when you gave me the Captain's uniform, you said that the boot style and sash embroidery were traditional, copied faithfully since the time of the Kingdom. I had hoped the Sharith might have kept the knowledge of Kä's location—?"

71

Dharak shook his head. "You must remember, Captain, that the loyalty of the Sharith is to Serkajon, not to the kings. That is the only reason I can give you for our not knowing about the other sword of rakor, the Kings' sword—you are *sure* it exists?"

"I'm sure," I said. "It's not surprising that, with Rika physically close and totally unique today, the memory of the other sword would fade. It was only in Eddarta, where the Lords have a rare talent for holding grudges, that the Kings' sword became a symbol of betrayal, important enough to be remembered through all these years."

"All these years—Kä," Dharak murmured. "Rikardon, you realize this may not be possible?"

"It's possible," I said, and stretched my arms wide to cover the shiver of doubt that followed that positive-sounding announcement. "If the Sharith have no further information about Kä, then there is only one other choice—I must consult a Recorder."

Dharak rubbed his eyes, another reminder of the late hour. Gandalaran lamps stood on shelves and small tables around the room—faceted glass chimneys that made the most of the light of the candles inside them. The candles were stubby; one flickered and went out while Dharak was speaking.

"There is a Recorder in Omergol," the Lieutenant said, talking through a half-suppressed yawn, "but I know nothing about his skills."

"His skills?" I echoed. "Forgive my ignorance, but I thought all Recorders do—what Recorders do."

"All those who have never had need of one think as you do, Captain," Dharak said. "There was an occasion in my youth in which my father sought out a Recorder, and I learned then that there are degrees of skill and special interests among them. You will require one of great skill who has some experience with the time of the Kingdom."

Maybe that's why Tarani refused to use her Recorder

72

training to find out if the sword exists, I thought. *She might have thought she just didn't have what it takes.*

"Who is the Recorder in Omergol?" Tarani was asking Dharak.

"His name is Somil," the Lieutenant answered, and laughed. "The caravan master who mentioned him—just a few days ago, in fact—does not prize him as a customer. It seems this Somil drives a hard bargain."

"I have heard of Somil," Tarani said, the awe in her voice causing us all to look at her. "At Recorder school, he was spoken of in whispers, as very old and highly skilled, but slightly scandalous. At that time, he lived— in Sulis, I believe. I wonder what brought him to Omergol?"

"I'll ask him," I said, standing up and stretching. "Day after tomorrow, in fact."

"You cannot force Keeshah to leave Yayshah now!" Tarani protested.

"Do I look *that* insensitive?" I asked, smiling and winning a return smile. "It sounds as if Somil may be able to help us and, if he has been moving around, it makes sense to try to catch him while he is in Omergol. There is only one problem—I'm not sure Keeshah will consent to my riding second on Ronar."

Thymas sat up straighter. "You want *me* to go with you?" he asked.

"If Ronar and Keeshah don't object," I said.

Thymas smiled ruefully. "I see; it is a test," he said. "Ronar's reaction to the idea will tell you whether I truly think of you as Captain of the Sharith."

"That's true," I said, "but as long as you're looking for reasons, let me help. I might want to give Dharak the opportunity to re-establish the command lines that have been stopping with you. I might want to get some distance between you and Dharak, to give you both some time to think. I might have some reservations— foolish and insulting as they would be—about leaving you and Tarani together in Thagorn overnight. I might

73

want the chance to get to know you better, without interference from the rivalry connected with Tarani or the memory of friction that Dharak and Thagorn keep fresh in our minds."

My voice had risen. I took a deep breath and made an effort to be calm, rather than angry and impatient.

"I might just need to go to Omergol, and want your company," I said.

Thymas stood up. "What time tomorrow?" he asked. "After lunch?" He nodded. "And no uniforms."

8

Thymas was right about one thing: I was trying to read Thymas through the actions of his sha'um. When Ronar stopped before Dharak's house and crouched to let me mount, I was half surprised and more than pleased.

Ronar was slightly smaller than Keeshah, but broad and sturdy. I eased my leg over the cat's hindquarters, tucked my knees into the angle formed by Thymas's, and used pressure against Ronar's flanks to ease the weight of my body on his pelvis.

Tarani and Dharak had walked out with me, but Shola had disappeared. She came out the front door of the house now, carrying leather pouches strapped together with rope. The Sharith called them travel packs; privately, I thought of them as saddlebags. She handed them to Thymas, who arranged the ropes across his thighs, laughing.

"This much food would see us all the way back to Eddarta," he said, then caught his mother in a warm hug. It took her a moment to react, then she hugged him back. When she stepped away from him, her face was glowing, and she flashed me a look of thanks that transferred some of the glow.

Dharak stepped up to us and put one hand on Thymas's shoulder, one on mine. "The Sharith wish you a safe and profitable trip," he said. "You will both be sorely missed."

I squeezed Dharak's arm. "Five days—six at the most," I promised.

Thymas grabbed Dharak's shoulder and said: "Father, when I get back . . ."

"We will do as the Captain suggests, son," Dharak said softly. "You and I will talk to each other."

We let Dharak go, and Tarani stepped up to take his place. Tarani and I had spoken our farewells during the night. Now she put her hands on my shoulders and kissed my cheek lightly, then repeated the gesture with Thymas—who brought his hands up as if to hold her, then lowered them without touching her.

Tarani moved around Ronar, tracing ridges of skin and patchy fur. "He is well healed," she said, and stroked the cat's jaw. "Care for them well, Ronar," she said, and stepped back.

At Thymas's silent command, Ronar stood up. Thymas and I rocked with the surging motion, then readjusted our positions for our own comfort and the cat's. I felt a little embarrassed that I had not even considered Ronar's recent injuries, especially since the earliest of them had been inflicted by Keeshah's claws and teeth. But the sha'um moved easily—if carefully—as he started for Thagorn's gate at a walk. Thymas and I waved at the group in front of the Lieutenant's house, then turned our faces forward.

Thagorn was busy, as usual. Repair crews worked at the wall of one of the barracks buildings that lined one side of the main avenue. Guards walked the upper level of the wall. From behind us, across the river, we could hear the noise of children playing and the barked commands of the cubs drilling their sha'um and themselves. People moved around, going to and from lunch, to and from duty stations.

All that confrontation last night was good for me, too, I thought, as I watched the activity we passed. *I feel more at ease, now that I don't have to worry about who knows what part of the story, and I guess it's true that "confession is good for the soul." When I finally admitted to Dharak and Thymas that it was my screw-up that lost us the Ra'ira, I stopped feeling so guilty about the past and started living frontwards again. I still haven't told anyone the truth about their "Visitor," but at least I'm down to only one lie—one that isn't hurting anybody, I hope.*

As Thymas and I rode toward the gate, I recaptured some of the sense of belonging I had missed the day before. As I became more in tune with the day's activities, I became aware of something not quite right, and searched through the moving people for that source of oddness. I saw it not twenty feet from the edge of the avenue—a man sprawled face-up on the ground. People were walking around him without a second look.

"Thymas, stop!" I said.

The boy turned his head in that direction, then leaned forward. Ronar started moving faster.

"What are you doing?" I demanded, leaning forward to keep my balance, but keeping my eyes on the man.

I found it hard to believe that the Sharith, who showed only fierce loyalty and caring to their own, were walking around what might be a corpse without a second look. As we passed the spot, I was relieved to see the man move his head, turning a sallow, ravaged face toward me. A scar stood out darkly on his right cheek.

"Thymas, it's Liden! He's sick. *Stop!*" I tugged at the boy's waist. Instead of calling Ronar to a stop, Thymas urged his sha'um to a faster pace, and freed one hand from Ronar's shoulders to grab tightly to my arms— effectively forestalling my half-formed plan to let go and just fall backwards.

Ronar's burst of speed took the gate guards by surprise. Though they put more muscle into swinging back the big double doors, the opening was barely big enough to let us pass when Ronar barrelled out of Thagorn.

I struggled against Thymas's hold, nearly upsetting us both. "Let it be, Captain!" he shouted over his shoulder. "Liden would not welcome your help."

"But he's ill!" I shouted back. "Why won't anyone help him?"

"His illness is too much barut," Thymas said. Ronar was slowing, and I had stopped struggling—but not arguing.

"That's impossible," I snapped, remembering the times I had *wanted* to get drunk and couldn't. "His body wouldn't let him do that."

Thymas was silent for a moment while Ronar came to a complete stop. There was sadness in the boy's voice when he said: "Cheral left for the Valley during the night. Liden's mind is—you probably understand better than I what he is going through. He is suffering, potentially violent. No one will help him until he asks—in a day or so. The shock has overcome his instincts for the moment, but they will not let him totally destroy himself."

During my last visit to Thagorn, I had met one or two "absent" Riders—men whose sha'um had left for the Valley, and who had taken residence and duty among the work crews for that year. They had been sad and subdued, haunted by the fear their sha'um would not return. I thought of Liden—tough and scrappy, full of laughter and pride—caught up in that despair, and shuddered.

How odd that I didn't remember those men while I was in Eddarta and Lingis, struggling with the same feelings, I thought. *I guess I expected more of myself—maybe I was lucky to have a real need for action to pull me out of that emotional morass.*

As if he could follow my thoughts, Thymas touched my knee lightly and said: "You see now that no Rider would blame you for what happened in the Darshi desert."

"Yes, I do see," I said. "And I'm really ready to go now."

He only nodded. We leaned forward again, Thymas grasping Ronar's back with his entire body, me clinging to the cat with my knees and to Thymas with my hands. Ronar started forward, gathered speed, and soon was running along the caravan trail that led around the tip of the Morkadạhl mountains and then north to Omergol.

The trip took us a day and a half, with frequent stops for rest and position-switching, and one night of sleeping under Gandalara's cloud-covered night sky. While the moon was overhead, the richly colored countryside faded to gray and black and silver; the moonless part of the night was nearly pitch black. I reached for Keeshah now and then, just to confirm our contact, but I didn't ask him for conversation. Settled in Thagorn, the two sha'um experienced a version of what they had known in the Valley. Much of Keeshah's surface thought was taken up with mate and den and hunting. I had disrupted that for him in the Valley. I had interrupted this new, halfway version the morning I left Thagorn because I needed his fully aware consent to my riding Ronar, which he gave grudgingly. Now I tried to keep out of his life as much as possible.

Thymas and I talked a lot during our rest periods, mostly about the trip to Eddarta. He asked me for more detail about the Valley of the Sha'um; I told him what I could, considering how little we had seen of any sha'um besides Keeshah and Yayshah.

"Perhaps I was wrong about your helping Liden," Thymas said, as we made ourselves comfortable for our night in the open.

"What do you mean?"

"You called Keeshah out of the Valley," the boy said, shrugging. "Perhaps you could show Liden how to call Cheral."

79

"I don't think so," I said. "The circumstances were . . . unique."

"And *you* are unique," Thymas said. "You and Tarani."

I looked at him in the quickly fading light, and felt vaguely disturbed that he wouldn't meet my eyes.

"I am no longer your rival, Rikardon," he said.

"And I was never yours," I answered. "Not for Dharak or Tarani. Not intentionally."

"I believe that," he said. "Good night."

We reached the outskirts of Omergol just at dusk. Having sent Ronar off to hunt and keep mostly out of sight, Thymas and I walked through the open gateway of the hillside city like any other two dusty travelers. Thymas's shock of thick, pale headfur caught a lot of attention—especially from women—as we moved up the stair levels from the older, less reputable parts of the city toward the higher and newer areas.

Omergol was built of its major export—pale green marble quarried from pits north of the city. Its beauty was dimmed in the dusky light and would return as reflected lamplight bathed the streets in a pale green glow. A lamp was already burning at either side of the doorway of our destination, the Green Sha'um Inn. It was located about halfway up the hillside, on our left.

"You say you know this place?" Thymas asked as we passed the entrance to the noisy bar and restaurant and approached the table beside the stairway.

"I know the owner," I said. "And he's a good source of information."

I asked the man behind the table for a room; he named a price and I paid it. With no need for discussion, Thymas and I turned back toward the bar.

"This is where I first met Bareff and Liden," I said, "and they were being less than courteous. *My* friend doesn't like *your* friends much; it will be best if he doesn't find out you—we—are Sharith."

We went through the open doorway and found ourselves enveloped in noise. The place was packed with people, most of them doing more drinking than eating. "I don't understand this," I shouted into Thymas's ear. "It was never this crowded before."

"Was *she* here before?" Thymas shouted back, waving toward the far end of the room.

The chaotic noise faded to a murmur, then died altogether as a young woman appeared through a doorway at the end of the long, wall-hugging bar—a doorway that had not been there on my last visit. As the noise settled down, so did the people who had been milling around, and I suddenly had a clear view of a small table against the wall across from the bar. Thymas and I made our way to it while the woman arranged herself on a chair in the middle of a small stage, and brought a flute-like instrument to her lips.

We forgot our hunger and thirst while she played. Her music was heart-wrenching and uplifting, terrifying and exalting. Markasset had heard the instrument played throughout his lifetime, but never like this. Thymas and I sat there, captivated, until the last note drifted into silence and she stood up, signalling the end of her performance. Then we joined the noise of approval, yelling, banging dishes, stamping the floor. When she had left the stage, we looked at each other as though waking from a daze. The better part of an hour had passed.

"Saw you come in, but couldn't get through the crowd," said a gruff voice behind me as a hand fell on my shoulder. "Welcome back."

I stood up to greet Grallen, the big, tough-looking man who owned the Green Sha'um Inn, but was still wearing the apron of a bartender. I introduced him to Thymas, who could only say: "Who is that woman?"

Grallen grinned, showing the spaces where teeth were missing in his lower jaw. "Her name is Yali—my wife's cousin. She has turned this place from a paying enterprise to a greedy man's dream. She will play again, later—meanwhile, we'll have some peace and quiet."

He waved at the column of people walking—some of them unsteadily—through the doorway. "What can I get for you and your friend, Rikardon?"

"Dinner and some information," I said. "Dinner first."

"On its way," Grallen said, slapped me on the shoulder, and headed for the kitchen.

Grallen showed up again in a few minutes to deliver our glith steaks and two glasses of faen, which were refilled more than once through the meal. Thymas and I were leaning back from the marble-tiled table, feeling that contentment unique to having eaten a good meal, when two Sharith walked into the room.

When those uniforms appeared in the doorway, everyone still in the dining room stood up and away from their tables.

Everyone but Thymas and me.

"What—?" Thymas said, and stood up, too—a few seconds after everyone else, so that the sound of his chair scraping on the floor drew everyone's attention to him. The smug looks on the faces of the two Riders vanished when they saw Thymas. The boy moved his head slightly. The Sharith moved quietly to an unoccupied table and sat down, removing their hats. There was a common sigh of relief, and a few puzzled glances in our direction, as everyone sat down again.

Thymas's air of contentment was gone; he was furious. "Visiting *any* city in uniform is strictly forbidden," he whispered fiercely. "And from what just happened here, I can see that this has been going on for a while. Dharak will turn to stone when he hears about this."

For my part, I was worried that Grallen had witnessed the exchange, and was much relieved when he came out of the kitchen, wiping his hands on a towel. I put my hand on Thymas's wrist, and the boy made an effort to compose himself.

Grallen picked up three glasses of faen at the bar and brought them over to our table, hooking a free chair with his foot. "Meal all right?" he asked as he sat down.

"Wonderful," I said.

"Good. Now—what is it you need to know?" He sipped his faen.

"I've heard there is a Recorder named Somil in Omergol," I said. "That is, he was here a few days ago. Is he still here, and do you know where I might find him?"

"I know him," Grallen said, gruffly. "I won't ask why you need to find the old lech." He gave us directions.

I gathered the old man lived in one of the better districts. Grallen drained his faen and stood up. "I need to get back to work—the second show crowd is starting to come in." He put his hand on my shoulder. "I have only one piece of advice for you about Somil; count your eyeballs carefully when you leave his place."

We stayed for Yali's second performance. If Thymas's pleasure was marred by his irritation with the Riders—who had left the place after only one glass of faen—it didn't show in the rapturous expression he wore while Yali played.

I had seen that look before—while Tarani danced.

We turned in and slept late the next morning. I took Thymas to Korredon's bathhouse, and he agreed the old man had magic in his fingers. After lunch, we wandered around Omergol until we found the house Grallen had described as belonging to Somil.

It was, as I had guessed, in the richest part of town, high on the hillside, with a small and fragrant garden lining a stone-paved walkway to the front of the house. The door was made of brass-fastened wood strips, decorative and heavy. It was opened, the second time I knocked, by a delicately beautiful girl whose head would not have reached my shoulder if she had stood on tiptoe.

She looked us over so carefully that I became worried she had figured out I had a fortune in gold coins in my belt. At last he spoke, clearly and softly. "Somil does not know you. What is it you wish?"

"I need the services of a Recorder," I said. "I am Rikardon; this is Thymas."

"Do you both wish to pay Somil for his services?"

The girl had large eyes and she tilted her face up to look directly at me.

"If he can do what I wish, I will pay him," I said.

"Then only you may enter," she said. She turned her dark gaze on Thymas. "You must go away."

I wouldn't want to be the one to say that to Thymas, I thought as I watched the boy's face darken.

"Thymas will stay with me," I said. "The information I seek is important to him, as well."

"But only one may seek," she said, as patient as a teacher with a child. "The one who pays."

The room behind the girl was the midhall which ran straight through to the back of the house, with rooms and stairways opening from it into the other parts of the house. A shadow moved on the part of the wood-panelled wall I could see.

"Then we will find another Recorder," I said, dragging Thymas away from the doorway, "to help us find Kä."

Thymas nearly had apoplexy, but the ploy worked. A tall and thin old man, his head totally bald, snatched the front door away from the girl and stepped up to the sill.

He smiled ingratiatingly and said: "Kä will cost you."

9

I reached into my pouch and brought out two of the Eddartan gold pieces, which I had earlier removed from my belt. I held them up, spread so that he could see that there were two.

"This is the price I'll pay," I said. "No haggling."

I knew full well, from the flash of eagerness the old man had let me see when he came to the door, that he would have done it for nothing. Ricardo was familiar with the passion of the educated for more knowledge. He was also familiar with the need of a shrewd businessman to maintain that image.

"Agreed," Somil said, and held out his hand.

I took Thymas's hand and put the coins in it.

"He will pay you—*after* I get the information I came for."

Somil drew his hand back, his wide-set dark eyes flashing from under his supraorbital ridge. "Who has told you I am a thief?" he demanded. His indignation was so sincere that I was taken aback.

"No one," I said, wondering if Grallen hadn't meant just that. "But someone *has* told me that not all Recorders have equivalent skills. Would you commission a set of dishes from a potter whose work you've never seen—and pay in advance?"

He made a choking sound, repeated it, then burst out

laughing. He stepped aside. "Come into my home, gentlemen, please. It is rare that I face a challenge and have a good laugh on the same day. A potter," he said again, laughing as we stepped through the doorway. "Indeed, a potter."

He led us through the midhall to the last door on the right, leaving the tiny girl to close the door. The room we entered was small and bare of any furniture besides four armchairs surrounding a small, tile-inlaid table. A second doorway, hung with a heavy tapestry, opened in the wall nearer the front of the house.

The three of us sat down in the chairs, and another young woman, dressed as the first was in a plain dark gown of a clingy fabric, brought us a cool drink flavored with herbs. As she bent over the table to place the third glass in front of Somil, his hand stroked her side, hip and thigh. She suppressed a giggle, looked at him with adoration, and fled the room.

I stared after her. Neither she nor the other girl could have been over fifteen years old.

I looked back at Somil and found his gaze directly on me.

"Whatever you may think of my lifestyle," he said pointedly, "I *am* a Recorder and I take the actual work of my profession as seriously as any of those who make the pretentious claim that virtue and skill are equivalent. There are operational rules which I will not violate. Only the Recorder and the seeker may be present," he said, a slight movement of his head indicating the tapestried doorway behind him. "Your friend may wait out here, if he likes, as long as he understands that to interrupt our session may be fatal to both of us."

"What do you mean, 'fatal?'" Thymas demanded.

"I mean fatal, as in dead or dying," Somil answered. "A Recorder builds a bridge, makes a connection with the All-Mind, and leads the seeker across. Both of us will be gone for the duration of the session. An interruption destroys the bridge, and the All-Mind has grown by two, do you see?"

"I see that if there is such danger, I should be the seeker," Thymas said flatly.

"No, I must go," I said, astonished that I had come to think of this mental exercise as a physical journey.

"There is another condition," Somil said. "If you knew precisely what you seek, you would have no need to seek it. Therefore you cannot tell me, *precisely,*" he emphasized, "what you want, and if I do not know it, I cannot guarantee it. I will do what you ask of me, and I will be paid, in good faith, for doing *only* what you ask of me. Any error in the request is your own responsibility."

"We agree to your terms," I said.

"Rikardon," Thymas protested. "I do *not* like this."

"Trusting, is he not?" Somil said. "Decide. Will you seek?"

His manner changed again in those last three words. When he had come to the door, he had been a showman. On entering this room, he had become a nuts-and-bolts professional. Now he was almost mystic, the holder of secrets, the guardian of truth.

The All-Mind may not be a god to the Gandalarans, I thought, *but the Recorders hold a place equivalent to that of "high priest" in Ricardo's world.*

I felt myself responding to the sense of ritual, and from Markasset's memory came the words which acknowledged Somil's transformation. "I will seek, Recorder," I said.

The old man rose silently and held back the tapestry for me to enter the inner room. Thymas grabbed at my arm, but I pressed his hand reassuringly, then removed it. I went into the dim room, which fell into near blackness when the door curtain swept back into place. I stood still until my eyes adjusted. The room was fairly small, with dark-paned lattice windows along one wall— the sole source of light. Against the doorway and inner walls were wide ledges with thick pallets. Somil was seated on one; he motioned me to the other.

"What do you seek?" he asked.

I remembered what he had said about asking the right question, so I thought a moment before I said anything. "Show me where Kä was built," I said, "and where it is today."

"One may follow from the other," he said, "but be warned: the All-Mind knows only what men have known. Do you understand?"

"I understand, Recorder."

He waved slightly, and lay full-length on his pallet. I followed suit, fighting a wave of panic. I had come this far because some instinct had told me that Somil *could* do this, but suddenly I had second thoughts.

"What troubles you?" Somil asked, and I jumped.

"How do you know I am troubled, Recorder?"

"You breathe shallowly; I see your hand clenching the edge of the pallet. You must be calm when we enter the All-Mind. Speak your fears, that I may put them to rest."

There was a richness to his voice, a timbre that was familiar—I had heard it in Tarani's voice while she worked for healing. It was strongly hypnotic, and I felt myself becoming more calm as Somil spoke.

I could resist this, I thought, *just as I can resist Tarani's skill. But if I let my non-Gandalaran mind resist this, I might make it impossible for Somil to make his link. I have chosen to use this Gandalaran power; I must let myself be Gandalaran.*

I let the peace wash over me.

"What do you fear?" Somil asked again.

"I fear being in your power," I said.

"I use my power only in your service," he said, and I believed him. "What else do you fear?"

"That you will see secrets in my mind," I said. I was vaguely conscious that my voice was slurred with relaxation. Part of me was surprised that I was speaking so frankly, but the lethargy had settled in too far to allow me to be alarmed.

"I will share with you what I see in the All-Mind, but I will not share your thoughts. What I learn of the All-Mind in your seeking is mine to keep or to give. Whatever I may learn of you will remain yours." He paused for a moment. "You are still afraid. Tell me."

"I fear the All-Mind will not admit me," I said.

"That has never happened," he replied, "but there is no danger in it. We would merely stop the seeking. Are you feeling more calm now?"

"Yes, Recorder."

"Then make your mind one with mine, as I have made mine one with the All-Mind . . ."

I stared into the darkness behind my closed eyelids and waited. There was a sliding sensation, a wrenching tug, and then I seemed to be in the midst of a network of brilliance.

. . . *We begin!* said Somil's mindvoice.

I felt no sense of my own substance. I was merely a location from which I could observe, but not act. The physical equivalent of that sensation would have disturbed me deeply, but here it promoted a feeling of security and calm in the face of overwhelming strangeness.

I knew I was "seeing" not the All-Mind itself, but a visual representation of it. The place that was me, enclosed and protected by the place that was Somil, began to move along one spoke of what seemed to be a geometrist's fantasy. Shining and translucent, cylinders of light joined an unplanned pattern of points that threaded through a three-dimensional shape that was roughly spherical. Some of the cylinders were short, others long. The only perceptible logic of the pattern was that the ragged, interconnected spines of light moved outward from the center of the sphere. Somil and I seemed to be toward the outer edge of the sphere, which was marked by an amorphous radiance into which the outermost cylinders disappeared. We had begun to move inward, seeking the congested core of the All-Mind.

I wondered if the All-Mind "looked" like this to everyone, or if this were Somil's interpretation of it, or mine.

It is your vision, Somil's mindvoice said, *and I thank you for it. I shall see it this way always.*

The shining spokes were everywhere. They flashed by us, the only source of awareness that we were moving. The spoke we followed joined another, and another, until we were enclosed in a shining, three-dimensional maze.

How do you find your way? I asked Somil.

Hush, he warned, *I must concentrate.*

Even though all my own perceptions came through Somil, I realized that I was observing independently. In an effort to understand what *he* was seeing, I "watched" Somil more closely, focusing on his mindvoice and closing off my own awareness of the glowing cylinders. I had felt as if I were floating beside the cylinders without "touching" them. Somil did seem to touch them; it was as if they were tracks which he rode, and he was holding me away from direct contact with them.

I forced my consciousness into closer bond with Somil, trying to see what *he* was seeing. I caught the barest glimpse, and my mind jerked backward, reeling from the impressions I had shared with Somil.

As if we had physical presence, my reaction pulled at Somil, snapping him away from the cylinder he was following. Our linked minds went spinning through the emptiness that was not black, nor white, nor even space, merely a place *between* shining cylinders. Panic and guilt and vertigo swept through me, so that I was barely conscious of Somil's mindvoice, speaking to me with surprising calm—surprising because, when I did sense the sound and focused on it, I could also sense fear in the Recorder.

"*Come closer, as you did then,*" he advised me. "*Join with me, or we are both lost.*"

Somil's voice soothed my panic. I did the mental equivalent of closing my eyes and hanging on to him for dear life, and our dizzying whirl slowed. I sensed, but did not watch, Somil reaching out for a cylinder, establishing a tenuous contact, and gradually guiding us along that contact. I knew when we were close enough to touch the cylinder, and fear churned up in me again.

"*It will not be the same,*" Somil assured me. "*We will touch only a single moment. I will not move again until you have withdrawn.*"

He waited until he knew I had control and was ready, then he "landed" on the cylinder.

I was standing at the edge of a harvested grain field, kicking at the dry dirt and worrying about next year's crop. The yield, and the income from it, had been the smallest ever. I hated the watermaster, but I knew he was right about the ground drying out. If I paid him for water, would next year's crop be bigger enough to give me more profit? Or would I end up like all the rest, owing him so much that, piece by piece, he would begin to own this stretch of ground that had supported my ancestors? What else could I do? We could move—I, and my wife, and our two daughters—but we could not take the land with us, and any land that would still grow crops was sure to be occupied. And I had no other skills. Visions of my family in rags, my girls working as household help or toiling in someone else's fields tortured me.

Somil pushed me gently away from the cylinder, and I came free of the memory I had shared with the nameless farmer. I had a moment of disorientation, a flash of anger, a devastating sense of loss, and then I was whole again and I understood what had happened.

"*How can you stand it?*" I asked the Recorder, as we began to move along this cylinder, aiming as before toward the center of the spherical mass of tangled light.

"I am trained for it," Somil replied. *"And it does not affect me in the same way. What you have experienced, I have only viewed."*

Professional detachment—it made sense. In the instant when I had recoiled, throwing us off-course, we had been traveling at what seemed to be tremendous speed, and Somil had been "dipping" into the cylinders, each one of which was the life memories of a single individual. By "looking" at those memories at intervals, Somil kept his bearings of "where" and "when" we were, and flashing instants of contact were all he needed to guide him. I had not been prepared for what I saw when I joined him, and those brief touches had been for me, as Somil said, a succession of different identities, men and women at all life stages, complete with problems and joy and grief and terror—some of the last my own, as I lost touch with myself and feared I could never regain my own identity.

"Will it be like that when we find Kä?" I asked. We were moving rapidly through the All-Mind now, but I noticed that we no longer swept toward the center, but were following spoke connections, roughly arcing around the densest part of the All-Mind.

"We have found it," he said, slowing. *"This woman lived in Kä,"* he murmured, *"born there to slave parents, lived all her life as a slave. She knows only that Kä is surrounded by desert."* We moved past a joining, glided along more cylinders. I sensed that Somil was concentrating deeply, so I kept quiet. *"More slaves,"* he said. *"Ah, here is a merchant . . . he thinks of Raithskar and Omergol as an equal distance away from Kä. Does that help?"*

"A little," I said. *"How much distance?"*

"Eight caravan-days," he said.

"That will help me find the general area," I said, *"but I was hoping for something more specific."*

The Recorder hesitated.

"What is it?" I asked.

"The answer to your earlier question," Somil replied. *"It is the common thing to allow you to share memory with someone who knew what you wish to know. Yet, in my experience, no one has been so profoundly affected by that sharing as you are. There could be danger for you in this."*

"There could also be great learning?" I asked.

His mindvoice did not hesitate. *"The most powerful kind of learning,"* he agreed. *"Will you seek in this manner?"*

I thought about it, and decided that, if I let myself in for this, I didn't want to do it twice, and I didn't want to waste the chance. *"Only if I may share memory with Zanek, the First King,"* I told Somil.

10

The Recorder's presence shivered with excitement. *"I will search for him,"* he said, and we headed more toward the center again, moving dizzyingly fast.

"Are you afraid I will change my mind?" I asked.

The Recorder responded to the words, but not to the intended humor. *"I sense your commitment to learn of Zanek,"* he assured me, *"and I know you sense my eagerness to share your learning. There is a time factor involved—we must leave the All-Mind soon."*

"But we've been here only moments!" I protested.

"So it would seem," he said, still guiding us rapidly along a shining spoke. *"But the mind and the body experience time differently, and our bodies suffer from our absence. When it is time, we shall go. I need no agreement from you in this; my judgment rules. Is that understood?"*

I was beginning to get excited as well. I did not know whether Zanek's memories would give me any more information than I already had about where I could find Kä today, but the prospect of getting to know the First King as a person, rather than a legend, was an attractive one. Before going to Eddarta, all I had known of Zanek was that he had organized the far-scattered cities of Gandalara into a peaceful kingdom. In Eddarta, my respect for his wisdom had tripled, as I learned that he had possessed the Ra'ira and had used its telepathic power only in beneficial ways—a testament to his strength and incorruptibility.

Yes, I decided, even if I had time for only a taste of the man's true nature, it would be worth it.

"*I understand,*" I assured Somil.

"*Good,*" he said. I noticed we had slowed our progress in the few seconds my deliberation had taken. "*Rikardon, meet Zanek.*"

Somil must have been exercising some undetectable control, because I didn't invest myself quite so completely in Zanek's memories as I had, for example, in those of the young and desperate farmer. Enough detachment remained for me to retain a sense of my own identity, so that what I saw through Zanek's eyes and in his self-knowledge had some of the quality of watching a live-action, all-surrounding movie. That detachment was amplified by the fact that I was not allowed to *become* Zanek, but was pulled along his lifememory by Somil. I shared moments of his experience that were sequential but not contiguous—rather like reading an intimate, anecdotal biography of the man. The final cause of difference between this sharing and the others was that I had some preconceptions about Zanek, and I was constantly comparing fact against expectation—with some startling surprises.

Zanek came from Raithskar.

And he was a Rider.

And it was he who had discovered what the Ra'ira could do. . . .

I was shaking inside, staring at the woman whose hand I held, shivering with the joy and the strangeness. I had shared thought before—did I not share every moment of my existence, now, with Skerral, the sha'um whose friendship I had won in the Valley? But it had never been like this, to see the thoughts of another person, to feel Mira's love reaching out to me. I had hoped for her caring, of course—I had brought the strange blue stone, discovered by my father in the rakor mine, as a betrothal gift. I put my hand over the pouch in which I carried the stone, felt its shape pressing into my palm and thigh.

Mira moved closer to me. We were sitting on the edge of the low stone fence that surrounded the vegetable garden behind her father's farmhouse. "Is something wrong, Zanek?" she said.

I knew, then, that she could not see my thoughts as I saw hers, and my wonder was such that I could not even speak to her. I fumbled with the drawstring of the pouch, hoping the presentation of the gift would make words unnecessary.

My hand was stilled by an awareness that Mira's father was approaching us. There was no word, no sound—but I knew he was behind me, and I stood to face him. He was a burly man, a farmer, unschooled and rough. It had taken no special skill for him to see how I felt about his daughter, or for me to see how little he approved of my feelings.

Mira had stood up beside me, her hand tightening on mine. Philon's sharp eyes had not missed the action, and I was swept up in a storm of emotion—anger with me and fear of losing Mira, jealousy, an unexpected sense of his own inadequacy in the face of my education, suspicious awe of my bond with Skerral, and through it all, determination that I should not be the one to claim Mira as wife.

I thought, he is stubborn and afraid, but he cannot rule Mira's life. I know she loves me, but she will not come to me willingly without his consent. He will consent—for his good, and hers, and mine—he will consent.

I believed that fiercely, as if holding my conviction strongly enough would convince Mira's father. Philon was moving toward us slowly, and I saw the change expressed in his features even as I felt it in his emotions.

The grim look faded from his face, to be replaced by one of resignation, mingled with confusion. His fear and jealousy was still reaching me, but faintly, as if they were being suppressed.

"I have it in mind, boy," the big man said, "that you want to marry my daughter."

Beside me, Mira caught her breath in surprise and fear.

"Yes, sir, and you have my promise to care for her well."

"Does she wish it?" he asked, then addressed the question directly to her. "Do you want to marry this landless wanderer, girl?"

"I want that very much, father," Mira said, strength and pride in her voice, her underlying puzzlement at the change in her father reaching me clearly.

"Then I'll—" He stopped, frowned.

I concentrated harder, thinking "You will consent. You will consent."

"I will consent," he said, then turned and walked away.

I stared after him, silent and terrified, until Mira pulled at my hand. "You have not asked me, you know," she said shyly. I could feel her surprise at her father's sudden attitude reversal fading. In its place was growing a joy so sweet and piercing that I could not bear it— because it was denied to me.

I could still feel an oddness from Philon's retreating figure. He knew what he had done; he understood the consequences, but he was beginning to wonder why he had done it.

I was beginning to know why, and the knowledge frightened me.

I turned to Mira and mumbled some kind of apology, softened the shock with a quick embrace, and ran away.

It was nearly a year later. I had run, not only from Mira, but from Raithskar, confused by the awesome mindgift I had acquired so suddenly. I had ridden from one end of the world to the other, at first driven by fear of my own power and then by curiosity. For I had found a sameness in all parts of the world—a physical pattern of less water and drier earth, a social pattern of envy and conflict between men and cities. I had learned to appreciate Raithskar, secure from attack by wild vineh because of its high walls, secure from attack by its neighbors because of the presence of the Riders, men who had dared to face the Alkhum crossing and the uncertain fate of the Valley for the sake of that rare prize, a sha'um friendship.

I had learned, too, that the gift was not solely mine, but linked to the strange blue stone, which no one had seen besides my father. When I had it with me, I could read the thoughts of other people; when I was more than a certain distance away from it, the skill disappeared. I had performed tests, and discovered that I could control another's thoughts, much more subtly than I had done with Philon. The power horrified me, and I had spent much time in learning to control my own thoughts, to prevent inadvertent influence over others.

I had returned to Raithskar with a firm purpose, and I had just presented that purpose to a meeting of all the Riders in the city. The Ra'ira, as I had come to call the blue stone, was in my pouch, and I scanned the thoughts of the members of the group. I saw some who saw my proposal as a means to personal power, and these names I noted to myself. For the most part, however, I was gratified to see that I had impressed most of them with my own sense of destiny, my conviction that we held the future of the world in our hands—and I knew that my words, and not my thoughts, had convinced them.

From Raithskar, the Sharith had scattered to cities and villages and isolated farmhouses on both sides of the world, carrying the message—you are not alone in your suffering; sharing, not conflict, is the only solution. The fact that the message arrived on the back of a sha'um was a subtle statement of power that required that the message be taken seriously. Representatives from almost every city and village had come to Raithskar—some out of fear, some out of curiosity, a few out of desperation—to meet with me.

It was the third day of the meeting, and the stiff formality of the first day had vanished. The group sat at or milled around the tables which had been set up in the city's square for this purpose and laid with refreshments. These representatives had agreed, in principle, on the need to share resources; most of them were now haggling over trade rates. Objections were shouted, quarrels settled with fists. Riders, stationed as guards around the square, looked at me for permission to interfere, but I withheld it. I moved around and through the crowd, my hand on the Ra'ira, and I searched for truth.

For the most part, the men who were speaking for their cities had honorable intentions. There were a few who were, in fact as well as in appearance, truly representing the ruling authority of their home cities. I felt a lot of outright greed and scheming in the crowd, but more frequently an undirected sense that the situation was a fair opportunity, if one could figure out how to use it.

At last, I called the group to order through the simple expedient of calling Skerral into the square and mounting him. All eyes turned to me.

"Go home," I said. "And take this message with you. A new age has arrived, one in which every Gandalaran will share, rather than take, cooperate rather than be conquered. I and the Sharith will be the body of law to enforce peace in the land—any man who takes arms against another endangers us all, and thus will take the risk of facing a sha'um.

"The city of Raithskar was gracious enough to host this meeting, at a tremendous cost in food and inconvenience. That will not be necessary again. My Riders and

I will start a new settlement, at the edge of the Great Pleth. Tell your people that anyone who is willing to work at farming or building is welcome to join us there—especially those whose land has dried to worthlessness.

"Within the next three moons, my Riders will come again to your cities, bearing word whether each of you here today will be permitted to represent your cities at future meetings. Most of you will be invited to the next meeting in six moons, which will be held in the new city, to be called Kä. But those of you who harbor secret thoughts of personal gain will be dismissed from representation, as will any successor with the same motives, until every settlement in Gandalara is represented by honest and dedicated people."

I resolved, as I rode from the square, to conceal myself near Raithskar's gate and make written notes of what I learned from the representatives as they passed through on their way to their homes. It would take some time to assure the honest representation I wanted, but I was sure it would happen. For now, I let Skerral carry me out through the gate; I lay forward against his furred back and let his joy in running lighten the weight of the responsibility I had undertaken.

Four years had passed, and everything had gone well. The Riders, whose loyalty to me and to my vision never ceased to touch me deeply, had barely begun to build the smallish settlement we planned when people started to arrive from the areas nearby. It had become quickly apparent that the city's growth would result in chaos if ungoverned, and I had suddenly become not only a builder, but an administrator, responsible for planning decisions and records maintenance—who had come, where they lived, what they promised Kä. The price of admission for everyone had been a portion of time or skill devoted to what was soon dubbed "government city," and Kä had been built with truly unbelievable swiftness. Water channeled from the Pleth turned the waste of white sand into a green and fertile oasis.

Three years after our arrival at Kä, Skerral had left me. Now it was more than a year since, and I was sitting in the sand block shelter in which the sha'um had slept, facing the terrifying thought that Skerral would not come back.

I reached into my pouch and drew out the Ra'ira. Not once, since the short-term experimentation in which I had indulged after the experience with Mira's father, had I attempted control through the Ra'ira, but I had used it often to see into the minds of others, with specific purpose: to find my enemies, and learn how to make friends of them; to detect problems before they festered beyond reasonable solution.

Now I contemplated using the power of the stone for my own gain. Perhaps, with its aid, I could reach through the blankness that blocked my contact with Skerral, and end this torturous uncertainty. It was my purpose, I told myself, merely to find out if he would return to me.

I lay down on the floor of the shelter, clutched the Ra'ira tightly in my hand, and projected my thoughts in search of Skerral. I found him in the Valley, with his mate and cubs. His mind was strangely different now, ruled by instinct and physical need, and I sensed an enviable contentment in him.

I also sensed that, while he did not think of me, he had not forgotten me. The mindlink we had shared was still there, suppressed though it was by the life needs which had drawn him back to the Valley. I realized then that I had deceived myself. It was long past the usual time when Skerral should have returned; I had already known, though could not admit, that whatever factors caused a sha'um to abandon his Rider had occurred for Skerral.

You are wrong, Skerral said clearly.

It was as if the thinking creature had lifted itself from

101

the animal and turned its face to look at me directly. I was shocked, and oddly shamed, as though I had been caught eavesdropping. My joy in renewing the mind-bond swept away those feelings for a moment, then was checked by my recognition of what the sha'um had said.

How am I wrong? I asked.

I choose, he said. *I will stay.*

Why? I asked, bewildered and not a little frightened. Had I found Skerral only to lose him again?

As was always the case, the sha'um was sensitive to my feelings as well as my thoughts, and sadness and resignation radiated from him as he answered me.

People need you, he said. *Not together.*

Understanding crushed down on me. Building and running a new city and a new government at the same time had been an all-consuming job, and my "runs" with Skerral had been infrequent these past few years. I had learned to accept a place in life which forbade intimate friendships—the Sharith thought of me as a part of them, but our tasks lay in different areas. Through all the increasing isolation, the sha'um's mind-presence had been comfort and support for me—the thought of living the remainder of my life without it was terrifying.

Please come back, I pleaded with the sha'um. *I need you.*

Still here, Skerral said. *In Valley.*

You mean we can still talk to one another, even though you're in the Valley and I am in Kä?

Yes, the sha'um answered.

I tried to believe it was possible, but I could not. The Valley would stimulate the sha'um's life instincts, gradually weaken and destroy our bond. And I would be alone.

Come back! I said desperately. *Come back!*

Skerral's mind recoiled from mine, shocking me into awareness. Unconsciously, I had been using the influence power of the Ra'ira, sending a message, not of need, but of compulsion.

Skerral, I am sorry! I told the sha'um, deliberately eliminating any taste of compulsion from the communication. *I did not mean—please, I do need you. Come back to Kä.*

No, Skerral said, and there was still a sense of greater distance between us. *Link will fade,* he said, agreeing with my earlier thought. *Better end now. Sorry.*

And he was gone, closed to me, totally immersed in hunting food for his family. Frantic with guilt and loss, I clutched the Ra'ira with the impulse to force a reopening of the link. Two things stopped me.

First, a glimmer of rationality considered the fact that compulsion had not affected Skerral earlier, and probably would have no effect now.

Second, my regard for Skerral finally found its way through the maze of need that had gripped me. In the Valley, Skerral had the close companionship of his family. His return to Kä would deprive him of that, and no substitute could replace it.

In spite of this terrible cost, above all personal needs and private horrors, one truth had never wavered: I was the first King of Gandalara, not solely by contrivance or by destiny, but by choice and commitment. Even had he come back, I could have spared little time for physical companionship with Skerral.

I resolved, in that moment, that no one—no man, and no sha'um—would ever be forced to face these choices again. There would come a time when a means to determine my successor must be detailed. Among those criteria would be a restriction: future Kings of Gandalara could not be drawn from the Sharith.

11

Somil pulled me away from Zanek, saying: "*We must go now.*"

In spite of our earlier conversation, I protested.

"*No! Did he ever marry, ever find any personal happiness? What did the Sharith say about the restriction he proposed? Did he ever see Skerral again, or share a mindlink?*"

Somil's mind carried me firmly and swiftly along the glowing spokes, outward from the center of the All-Mind. "*We cannot stay,*" he said, with true regret. "*But I sense that you already know the answers to your questions.*"

I considered that. Yes, I did—they were implicit in what I had learned about Zanek and his life in those few contacts. He would remain isolated, bestowing all his love and energy on the newly founded Kingdom. I knew that Skerral's withdrawal had been final; it was only sympathy for the lonely and dedicated man that had let me hope for any change there. And as for the Sharith . . .

Suddenly the Bronze and the other sword made sense. The Sharith had been, in Zanek's time as now, fiercely proud. Zanek would have known that, even with full explanation of the reasons for his action, the Sharith might have seen his prohibition of future Sharith Kings as an ungrateful and disloyal act, and a waste of the best resources available.

He would have taken great care to reaffirm the importance of the Sharith to the Kingdom. Had I been Zanek . . .

I could see the plan progressing secretly through the later years of Zanek's life. Using only people whose silence he could trust—as only Zanek could know such a thing—he would have ordered the forging of two swords made of rakor, and he would have commissioned the huge bronze plaque, possibly traveling to Eddarta personally to guide the imprinting of its special message.

Back in Kä, he would have begun his search for a successor, touching the minds of young people, seeking not only a basic mindgift but integrity and responsibility. Those he thought suitable, he would have brought before the Bronze. The person who read it most easily and was moved by its message to vow sincerely the commitment required to be King, would have been chosen by Zanek as his successor.

He would have called a formal, festive meeting to announce who his successor would be. He would have carried the Ra'ira in plain sight, as he would have done for some time. It must have been seen in his possession frequently throughout the years, but Zanek's carefully limited use of its power would have allowed it to gain the reputation of only a symbol. The room would have been large, palatial. One wall would have needed full covering by movable drapes, and there must have been a platform or table, also draped. The civil leaders of the city, representatives of other cities, and several Sharith (including the Captain, of course) would have been present in the audience hall.

Zanek would have restated the purpose of the meeting—to inform the Kingdom of the identity of his successor. (It is not unlikely that the Captain would have moved slightly at that point, looking over the Sharith in the room, speculating on which man would be the next

King.) The King would have given the criteria for his choice: a person young enough to receive extensive training before assuming responsibility; a person filled with commitment; a person who was *not* a Rider. (Shock would have run through the company, more than the Sharith having expected that the choice lay with them.)

Zanek would have recounted his personal tragedy, but only in passing. He would have stressed the point that the Kingdom needed both leadership and power, and that King and Sharith must be forever separate, but forever bound to one another. He would have called the Captain to his side, then, and undraped the wonderful, valuable, shining swords, displayed so that the entire company could see them. Perhaps Zanek would have offered the Captain his choice of swords, then gripped the hilt of the other for himself. Zanek would have given everyone time to see the significance of the symbolism— King and Captain with identical swords unique to the Kingdom—and then he would have asked the Captain to stand against the draped wall for a moment, with the rakor sword having replaced the bronze sword in his baldric.

The Captain would have stood there proudly while Zanek placed the Ra'ira on a small table toward the other end of the wall, leaving a large blank space in the center of the drape. Then Zanek would have faced the company again, and called the name of his chosen successor. The boy would have appeared from the far doors, and walked with quiet dignity among the staring eyes.

Zanek would have uncovered the Bronze then, and asked the boy to read aloud the first part of the message hidden in the mass markings:

I greet thee in the name of the new Kingdom.

From chaos have we created order.
From strife have we enabled peace.
From greed have we encouraged sharing.

Not I alone, but the Sharith have done this.
Not we alone, but the Ra'ira has done this.

Zanek would have told the group that there was more of the message, that the reading of it would be part of the test for those who would follow himself and the boy, and that it clearly directed the respect of the King for the Sharith. He would have said that, on the day the boy took from Zanek's hand the blue stone and the gleaming sword—on that day, the boy would be King of Gandalara.

Thus Zanek would have vested such dignity and value in the Sharith that being prohibited from the Kingship would have seemed less insult than privilege.

"*I require your attention,*" Somil's mindvoice said, sounding weary.

I withdrew from my speculation about Zanek, as sure of what I had guessed as if I had truly shared that memory. We were at the edge once more, the intensely bright core of the All-Mind far behind us; only the amorphous, concave, intangible inner surface of the glowing sphere looming close.

"*Yes, Recorder,*" I said.

"*Hold closely to me as we leave the All-Mind,*" Somil ordered, and I obeyed. "*I shall withdraw our minds from the All-Mind,*" he said. Brilliance faded into absolute darkness. "*And mine from yours,*" he added. I seemed to slide into something very cool, and an emptiness appeared where Somil's mindvoice had been.

I opened my eyes. The dimness of the room seemed to have a different quality. I looked around and found that no daylight came through the narrow windows, but a shaded lamp stood on a ledge below them, casting only a little candleglow into the darkness. I was very cold; my arms responded sluggishly, the skin tingling, as I brought them over my chest to enfold some warmth.

"Do not rise," Somil said. His voice was weak, but still had that commanding quality. I saw his arm reach out to a table near him, and heard a soft, mellow tone—a chime of some sort.

The drape was moved aside immediately, and the two young girls hurried in, one carrying a tray of food, the other a fully bright lamp. They set down what they carried and came to kneel beside us. The girl who had opened the front door tended me, massaging my arms and legs briskly, helping me to sit, offering me a dish of steaming rafel. Hunger nearly doubled me over when I smelled the food, and I ate it greedily. Somil was attacking his dish with equal ardor.

"How long—" I began.

"It is nearly dawn," the girl beside me said. "It is the longest dear Somil has been away; we feared greatly for you both." The girl beside the Recorder did not touch him as he ate, but her eager expression made me think that a massage and a hot meal were not the only rituals of renewal Somil demanded after a trip to the All-Mind. The expression changed to surprise and hurt when Somil pushed her gently off his resting ledge and asked both girls to leave the room. They protested, but went.

Somil looked at me across the food tray.

"It is rare that I learn so much of the seeker," he said slowly, "or that what I do learn only leads to greater mysteries. It is fitting that you should seek out Zanek—for are you not, as he was, a man committed to his destiny?"

My hands tightened on the bowl I held.

"Do you *know* what my destiny is?" I whispered, but my hopes fell when he shook his head.

"The future is yet unformed," Somil said. "I cannot say why or how it is given to some men to guide its forming, but I have seen it, in Zanek. I have met it, in you."

There was a commotion at the doorway, the voices of the girls protesting and another voice speaking angrily— Thymas. "I hear their voices," Thymas said. "I have to talk to him. Stand away!"

"Can you rise?" Somil asked me urgently. I nodded.

"Then go and calm him," he ordered. "He must not enter this room." I stood up, a little shakily, and stretched my arm to the wall for support as I moved toward the doorway. "I say again, Rikardon, that what I have learned of you remains yours."

I turned at the doorway and said: "Thank you, Recorder." Then I shoved aside the tapestry and stepped into the anteroom, colliding with one of the girls who blocked the doorway.

Thymas had drawn his sword, but the girls had called his bluff and held their ground. Relief flooded into his face when he saw me.

"Rikardon, we have to go back to Thagorn. Right away." He put away his sword, without apology, and drew a many-folded slip of paper from where it had been tucked into his belt. There was a solid deliberateness to his actions that was more alarming than his normal barely controlled wildness. "The messenger found me here just after nightfall," he said. "I did not dare disturb you, but when I heard voices . . ."

I took the paper from him—the pattern of its folds was typical of a message sent in the breast-packet of a maufa, the Gandalaran message bird—and opened it, stepping away from the door as Somil emerged from the inner room.

It was a hasty scrawl that said as much, and was as unsettling, in its disarray as in its words:

> *Thymas*
> *You are Lieutenant.*
>
> *Dharak*

"Is this Dharak's writing?" I asked the boy. He nodded. "Then let's get going," I said.

"Not before I am paid," said Somil. He was leaning against the wall, one arm around a girl, the other extended toward us.

Thymas muttered something, drew out the two gold coins, and dropped them on Somil's open palm. "Thank

109

you," Somil said, closing his hand around the coins. "Do come again, if I can be of service." His words and manner were cynical, but I heard sincerity in them, and touched his shoulder in farewell before I turned to follow Thymas out into the street.

We dashed into Grallen's hotel and stayed only long enough to retrieve our bags and pay the extra night's rent on the room. Then we ran down the stair-stepped entry avenue and out of Omergol. Ronar was waiting for us; we mounted and started for Thagorn.

Keeshah, I called. *Is anything wrong? What's happening there?*

I had wakened him; his mindvoice was sleepy. *Nothing wrong,* he said. *Female always hungry.*

I let him drift away, back into his sleep.

"Keeshah can't tell me what's wrong," I said. "Yayshah's fine; that's all he cares about right now."

"Thank you for asking," Thymas shouted back.

I could feel the tension in the boy's body.

"Lighten up," I urged him. "You'll wear Ronar out before noon."

Only consideration for his sha'um could have penetrated his fear, but I felt him nod and make an effort to relax. I patted his leg in an effort to offer some comfort.

I knew what he was thinking, and it scared me, too. The only way I knew for Thymas to become Lieutenant was through Dharak's death.

12

Ronar, of course, was sensitive to Thymas's distress and urgent need to reach Thagorn, and the sha'um pushed himself to his limits. Thymas had left Somil's house briefly, during the night, to gather supplies for the trip, and I could only admire the common sense of his planning. The bags we had retrieved from the Green Sha'um Inn contained a small portion of food for him and me—cooked meat, bread, small fruits—but by far their major load was in chunks of raw meat wrapped in oiled cloth. They were no more than mouthfuls for Ronar, but in combination with a recent full meal, they were adequate to sustain a minimum energy level in the sha'um.

We ran straight to Thagorn, taking frequent but very short rests. The shock of Thymas's news had driven out the fatigue I had felt on returning from the All-Mind, but it caught up with me quickly, so that I spent the greater part of the trip in an unsatisfying half-doze. At midmorning of the next day, a shout from Thymas opened Thagorn's gates for us, and Ronar delivered us to the door of Dharak's house.

We slid to the ground from the sha'um's back as Shola came running out the front door. As anxious as Thymas was to get some answers, he took a moment to caress the panting cat in gratitude for his effort. Then he turned to

111

meet his mother and hold her tenderly until the spasm of sobbing passed.

Tarani waited in the doorway, greeting me with a nod and a sad smile. Shola took Thymas's hand and led him into the house, Tarani moving ahead of them. I followed.

Dharak was in a corner of the room that served as a parlor. He was sitting very still and looking out the lattice-paned window at the river. What he was *seeing* was beyond our guessing. His face was smooth and blank. Only the slight, regular, usually unnoticed movements of breathing told us he was alive.

Thymas went slowly to kneel by his father. He touched the thick white hair, so like his own, smoothing it back from the pointed widow's peak in the center of Dharak's forehead. He pressed the old man's hand and spoke his name. There was no response.

Without moving from his father's side, Thymas whispered: "What happened?"

Shola clasped her hands tightly. "He flew into a mad rage," she said. "He blundered about the house, striking walls and tables—not intending damage, I think, but simply not caring what was in his way. He went to his desk and wrote that note to you, then screamed for Bareff until he came. After he had given orders for the letter to be sent, he . . . faded to the way you see him now.

"He goes where he is led, eats and relieves himself when directed, sleeps—or, at least, lies quietly abed—when he is told." Her hands began to twist together, as if they were doing it without her knowledge. "I am so glad you have returned, Thymas. It has never been like this before—terrible, yes, but not like this."

"Before?" I echoed. "This has happened before?"

"Not this precisely," Shola answered. "But yes, of course—this is not the first time Doran has left for the Valley of the Sha'um."

Thymas jumped to his feet. "Doran gone? But it is too

112

soon. I remember the last time—it was only five years ago, was it not, mother?"

She nodded, and burst into sobs again. Tarani moved to her and put an arm around her shoulders; the older woman leaned gratefully against her.

A gnawing feeling had attacked my stomach and was working its way toward my toes and fingers. I ignored it, in full confidence that it would have its say soon.

"You yourself told me," I said to Thymas, "that the sha'um don't make their visits to the Valley on an absolutely predictable schedule. There is no calling Doran back. Take this," I said, pulling the many folded letter from my belt and giving it to him, "and find Bareff. You'll need to make plans."

The boy took the paper, nodded grimly, and left the room.

"The letter," Shola said, "I could not see what was in it before Dharak gave it to Bareff. What was in it?"

"Dharak named Thymas Lieutenant," I said gently. She gasped with surprise, and I touched her hand. "He may have meant the appointment to be permanent," I said, "but I doubt it. It sounds to me as though he knew he was not going to be able to function, and he wanted to give Thymas a sign of his confidence in him. When Doran returns, so will Dharak."

She caught my hand and clung to it. Her face showed the strain of her grief and fear; her eyes seemed to have sunk even farther under her prominent supraorbital ridge, and there was a grayish cast to her skin. "I am grateful you are here, Captain," she said, and went across the room to sit quietly by her husband.

Thymas burst into the room, Bareff hard on his heels. "I met Bareff coming to report to me," Thymas explained. He looked into my face and narrowed his eyes. "I think you have guessed the news he brings."

I sighed. "A lot of sha'um have left for the Valley in the past few days, right? Some of them much earlier than expected? Most of them older, sha'um who have been to the Valley at least once before?"

It was Bareff who answered. "The men were in all divisions, so it took us some time to notice the coincidence." He shrugged. "Figuring out *why* was the easy part."

Tarani moved into the center of the group, her manner defiant. It was clear to me that she had figured out what was happening, and had been preparing for this moment. "Yayshah was promised shelter until her cubs are delivered," she said, facing Thymas. "He spoke for the Sharith; we expect you to honor his word."

Before Thymas could answer, I asked Tarani: "When will the cubs be born?"

She hesitated a moment, and did not turn around when she answered. "I cannot say for certain."

"Two days?" I pressed. "A seven-day? A moon?"

She whirled on me then. "As long as it must be," she snapped, "we shall stay in Thagorn."

"Bareff," I asked, "how many sha'um are gone?"

He spent a second or two in thought, then answered. "Twenty-two."

"That's more than a fifth of all the sha'um in Thagorn, Tarani," I said. I gestured at Dharak. "More than a fifth of all Riders—disabled from their duty, disturbed and miserable. What's more," I added, unsure whether either Thymas or Bareff had considered this, but needing to make my point with Tarani, "the season is wrong for their going. The females are bearing now; they won't tolerate mating for several moons. That means the sha'um will be gone for a longer time than usual, and there is a greater chance they won't return."

"Is Yayshah to be blamed for that?"

"Not 'blamed,'" I said. "But I believe her presence here caused it, by stimulating the physical need of the sha'um to seek out mates. So far, only those who have felt it before have been susceptible. The first to go would have been those who were closest to their regular time

114

but, as you heard, Doran might have waited two more years, but for Yayshah. The longer we stay, the more the normal pattern will be skewed."

Thymas spoke up. "My father understood, when he granted the shelter you requested, that the effect of a female sha'um in Thagorn could not be predicted." He reached out, touched Tarani's arm, dropped his hand. "You and Yayshah are Sharith now, and must consider the good of all. I will support Dharak's word, if you require it, at whatever risk to the rest of us. But I ask you to release us from his promise, and take Yayshah away from here."

Tarani seemed to consider his request for a moment, then she shook her head. "Nothing is worth the cost of Yayshah's cubs—to force her to travel now would be dangerous for all of them." There was an odd trembling in her voice.

"Then it is settled," Thymas said, his shoulders slumping. He looked at his father with pity and fear. "Yayshah shall stay."

"For one more day," I said. "We will depart Thagorn tomorrow morning."

I did not give Tarani a chance to voice the protest she obviously intended.

"You said that asking Yayshah to move 'might' be dangerous for her cubs, Tarani. That possibility must be weighed against the certainty of further disruption of Thagorn. The promise of shelter here was mine, as well, but I'm Captain and responsible to and for the Sharith. Tell Yayshah we have to go."

"She cannot move," Tarani said flatly, her anger barely controlled.

Keeshah, I called. *I need to see what you see.*
Yes, he agreed.

I reached out to him and blended into the closeness that was so sweet and pure and stirring that we could share it only for brief moments. For a few seconds, I was part of him, receiving the same sensory input, feeling

115

the complicated blend of pride and contentment and good-natured grumpiness the presence of his mate stirred in him.

I saw Yayshah. She had torn and smashed and otherwise cleared away the ground cover and low bushes in a small area, to hollow out a sleeping nest. It was an obvious—and obviously unsatisfactory—imitation of the den in the Valley, where the taller, denser growth had provided a cavelike shelter. Keeshah was in the den, looking up as Yayshah lumbered through the opening. She was huge now, and she walked with a rocking motion to compensate for the balance shift caused by her swaying belly.

She came into the den, crouched awkwardly to rub her cheek and ear along Keeshah's shoulder, and flopped down on her side with her head across his hind legs. Keeshah stretched and yawned, kneaded her back gently with his forepaws, and relaxed again.

I broke the contact, both saddened and encouraged by what I had seen and warmed, as always, by the moment of closeness with Keeshah.

"Yayshah can walk," I said. "We will move slowly, both of us riding Keeshah, and stop frequently to let Keeshah hunt. If Yayshah's time comes, we will stop wherever we are, and care for her. But we *leave* Thagorn as soon as possible."

"She will not go," Tarani said again, trembling.

"She will go if you are convinced it is necessary," I replied. "Tarani, consider how deeply her *wishes* are affecting you. Her instincts demand a den—but if her instincts were all-powerful, she would never have left the Valley. Look beyond what she *wants* and try to see what she *needs*. Moving will make her unhappy, but I think the three of us can keep her—and the cubs—safe."

I had taken Tarani's hands in mine, trying desperately to convince her. I felt a deep and very personal commitment to the Sharith. I had been through, too recently, the abandonment of a sha'um to be the cause of

116

it for even one more Rider. I had put off our departure until morning out of a simple need for rest and for giving the sha'um a chance to get used to the idea.

I waited for Tarani to decide. If she refused to lead Yayshah out of Thagorn, there was only one other recourse—ask Thymas and the other riders to drive her out. I was not sure I could ask them to do that. I was not sure they would do it. I *was* sure that, no matter how I felt about the matter, Keeshah would defend her.

Please, Tarani, I begged silently. *Please understand.*

Her answer surprised me. She straightened her shoulders, withdrew her hands from mine, and said: "As Thymas said, I am Sharith now; as Captain you have the right to command this, and I will do as you say." She turned and walked out of the room and the house.

That will get us moving, I thought, *but this trip may be more uncomfortable for me than for Yayshah.*

"On behalf of the Sharith, I thank you, Rikardon," Thymas said, with more feeling than might be expected from the formal words. "I hope you will have not cause to regret your choice. We will, of course, provide whatever you need for your journey. Where will you go?"

"Toward Raithskar," I answered. "It may be possible to get there before the cubs arrive." I glanced at Dharak, thinking of Thanasset and looking forward to seeing "my" father again. "Shola, Thymas—I *am* sorry."

Thymas smiled—a little shakily at first, but finally with a glimmer of true good humor. "You made a sincere and reasoned judgment that happened to be a mistake," Thymas said. "Learn the lesson you tried to teach us, and do not accept more blame than you deserve."

"And please," added Shola, "remember the good you have done, as well." She stroked her husband's arm. "Dharak will come back to us when Doran returns," she said, projecting—or pretending—absolute sureness. "Thymas will be a better leader in the meantime, because you showed him his father's confidence in him."

117

Thymas's mother stood up and held out her arms to me. I embraced her; she stretched upward to kiss my cheek.

"You and Thymas have had a hurried and tiring trip back from Omergol. Rest now," she said. "I will see that food is packed for your journey."

13

I would not care to relive the hour, just after dawn of the following day, in which Tarani and I convinced Yayshah and Keeshah to leave their den. Keeshah came outside readily, but with questions and dread in his mind.

Why go? he complained. *Comfortable. Cubs? Female? Safe?*

I think so, Keeshah, I said. *We'll take every care we can.*

Female unhappy, he predicted, with admirable understatement, and added, with a sense of resignation and forbearance: *All unhappy.*

Yayshah had stayed inside, and Tarani and I stepped through the opening. The interior of the den was dim, but the outline of the female was clear and huge, her eyes shining with reflected light.

Yayshah backed away from Tarani, pressing against the deepest wall of the enclosure. Her teeth were bared and her ears flat against her head.

"You see her eagerness," Tarani said sarcastically, then focused her attention on the sha'um. She walked foward slowly, making a low and melodious sound. Yayshah growled. I checked my impulse to reach out and drag Tarani back.

I might have questioned the quality of the link

between Tarani and Yayshah, and wondered whether the cat's protective maternal instinct might override that special bond, so new to both of them. But I recalled other situations in which I had asked Tarani to face danger—now, as then, I reminded myself that she had accepted the task, and I had no choice but to let her accomplish it in her own way.

All the reasoning in the world could not keep me from crossing my fingers as the woman approached the sha'um and extended her hand toward the cat's muzzle.

Tarani's voice grew louder, and I detected the vibrancy that was always present when she used hypnotic, soothing sounds to assist the effectiveness of her illusions. Tarani was trying to calm Yayshah and ease the trauma of leaving her carefully prepared den, but she wasn't trying to force her will on the sha'um.

Nobody *forced* a sha'um to do anything.

The female hissed and raised a paw. I tensed and grabbed the hilt of my sword, but the paw only touched Tarani's shoulder and rested there. The girl swayed from its weight, then steadied, and put both her hands underneath the sha'um's jaw, stroking backward. Her voice never ceased its humming as she moved closer, brought her other shoulder under the cat's chin, lifted her arms to embrace the thick, furred neck. The glittering of Yayshah's eyes vanished, and I caught the movement as her ears pricked forward.

Cat and woman released one another, and Tarani backed toward the opening, still humming, inviting and drawing Yayshah with her outstretched hands. I retreated to make way for them. When Yayshah's head appeared in the rounded, green-bordered entryway and her eyes caught the sun, she balked. She lifted her head and made a sound that lifted the fur on my arms and neck, a shrieking roar that was unmistakably mournful, and vanished from the doorway.

A growl sounded right behind me, and Keeshah shouldered me aside. He was more gentle with Tarani, nudging her with the flat of his forehead, but he pushed her out of the way, too, and went into the den.

I will bring, Keeshah said.

Tarani looked at me, her face grim and sad. "She is so afraid, Rikardon."

"It's all right," I said. "Keeshah will bring her out."

I reached for her hand, but it lay unresponsively in mine as we peeked into the den. It was crowded, with both sha'um standing, but Keeshah had moved around until he stood beside the female, pressing against her. He turned his body until she was between him and the door, and started edging toward us. The cub-laden female may have outweighed Keeshah, but she was confused and frightened; he was basically bigger than she, and he had a definite purpose. In a few seconds, she had no choice but to come out into the open.

We gave Yayshah time for her eyes to adjust to the light, then Tarani and I walked to Thagorn's gate. Keeshah stayed near his mate, often with his side pressed tightly to hers for comfort, as we left the city.

The whole contingent of Sharith had massed in the barracks yards, and watched us come down the hillside. Thymas offered his hand. I gripped it and squeezed his shoulder, unable to spare much attention from the sha'um and knowing that he would understand. Tarani was totally preoccupied with Yayshah, whose irregular step and quick starts displayed her continued nervousness.

Shola and Thymas walked beside us the last few steps toward the gate. Tarani led the sha'um on through, but I paused.

Shola handed me the filled travel bags, which I slung over my shoulder. "Give Tarani my thanks and good wishes, Captain," she said, "and tell her my home and . . . and my heart are open to her."

I hugged her. "This comes from both of us," I said. "I know your message will please her."

121

"With all that has happened," Thymas said, "I have not heard what you found out about Kä."

"I know where to start looking," I said. "There was more—it will make a good story for the next time we meet."

"I hope it will be soon, Captain," the boy said.

"As soon as possible," I agreed. "Goodbye, Lieutenant."

I passed out through the gate, trotting to catch up with Tarani. We led the sha'um along the road, over the hill toward Omergol. After an hour or so, we stopped to rest. When Yayshah had flopped down and slipped into a light nap, Tarani sighed and sagged down to sit on the ground. Keeshah nosed around restlessly, and silence stretched over the roadside clearing.

"I had to make this choice," I said, at last.

"I see that," Tarani answered. "But you were correct about Yayshah's effect on me. I wanted that den as fiercely as she did. I will need some time, Rikardon, to reconcile the rightness and the pain of your choice."

"That's only fair," I said, and turned my attention to planning the trip.

Yayshah's ravenous appetite and unquenchable thirst required us to stay out of the desert, which left us with only one possible route. We followed the caravan road around the tip of the Morkadahls and stayed in the hillside country all the way north, past Alkhum to the low hills from which the Great Wall loomed upward. Our travel pattern was simple, too—we moved until Yayshah stopped, started again when she was refreshed.

At first, Tarani and Keeshah had to reconvince the female sha'um every time we moved from a camp. After a day or so, however, she relinquished her sullenness and seemed actually to enjoy the short spells of exercise.

Tarani and I rode Keeshah occasionally, but Yayshah moved slowly enough that we walked most of the time, sending Keeshah ahead to a likely stopping place, and letting him greet us with Yayshah's fresh-killed snack.

Tarani's mood lightened, but she remained thoughtful and a bit distant, and I was reluctant to push. I helplessly watched Yayshah as her belly grew until it nearly dragged the ground, and still detected no sign that the cubs were ready to meet the world. Paradoxically, as I became more anxious, Tarani became more confident. She said that Yayshah's concern had relaxed as she sensed her cubs were not suffering in the travel, and that she would know when the time was near. No matter where the cubs were born, Tarani said, the actual delivery would be guided by Yayshah's strongest instincts. Tarani never failed to add that, while Yayshah had adapted to the circumstances, she still longed for a dark and cozy den in which to greet the children.

I was so absorbed in the process of traveling, and with anxiety over Yayshah's condition and Tarani's distance, that I was surprised to waken one morning and recognize the familiar farmland that lay northeast of Raithskar. We had spent the moonless pre-dawn hours in a grove of fruit trees.

"We're nearly there," I told Tarani, "and game will be scarce from here on out. If you and Yayshah will wait here, Keeshah and I will ride ahead to the city, and bring food back."

"How long?" Tarani asked.

"Only a few hours," I said. "Will Yayshah be all right?"

The girl knelt beside the cat, laid her hands on the swollen belly. The skin jumped with inner movement, as it had done with increasing regularity during the past few days, and I thought: *It can't be much longer.*

As if she had read my mind, Tarani said: "It is nearly time. She cannot say how soon, but soon."

I looked around. The sheer cliff the Gandalarans call the Great Wall rose from its base only a few miles away to disappear in the cliffs above. I could hear the distant roar of the Skarkel Falls, might be able to see its source, but for the cloaking mist sprayed up by the crash of the water into the deep pool at the base of the Wall.

"Now that we have hit farmland, there will be no real shelter for her," I said. "Keeshah's house, in my father's yard, is the most suitable place I know. Can she make it that far?"

Tarani closed her eyes.

"Yayshah will try," she said, and turned a serious face toward me. "Please do not leave us."

"Won't she need food?" I asked.

"She wishes it, but does not require it," she said. "At least, not until after she delivers. It is more important that her mate be close by her now."

I set aside the homesickness that had nearly overwhelmed me, and we moved on together, causing no little stir among the people we passed along the way. For most of the morning, we moved cross-country, seeing only field workers and farmers. Toward noon, however, we struck the hard-packed caravan road that would take us directly into Raithskar. Had Keeshah and I been alone, we would have traveled parallel to the road, to ease the burden on the travelers who guided vlek-drawn carts or caravans of the pack animals. But Yayshah, moving ever more clumsily, was my chief concern, and the four of us took advantage of the smooth roadway, taking up nearly its full span.

Word of our approach might have reached Raithskar ahead of us, had anyone who saw us been able to break away. We were followed by a fascinated crowd of people who only served to make Yayshah more nervous. We moved through the open gateway into the marketplace, scattering surprised and terrified people. Yayshah had begun to make a moaning sound deep in her throat, and Tarani urged haste. Keeshah supported the female on one side; Tarani and I leaned against shoulder and hip on the other, less helpful than encouraging.

I breathed a sigh of relief when we turned into

Thanasset's street, and I shouted to Tarani that it was only a little further. The door of the solid, two-story house opened and Milda, Markasset's aunt, came out, obviously in search of the source of the crowd noise. When she saw us staggering toward her, her mouth flew open momentarily, then she snapped into action.

"Thanasset, come out here," she shouted, and ran to open the large gate into the garden.

Markasset's father appeared in the front doorway, his silhouette registering shock for only an instant. Then he was behind Tarani, helping to support Yayshah's shoulder. The crowd of us would not fit through the gateway, but Yayshah had seen the square building made of clay brick, and she staggered toward it under her own power. Either Tarani had told her what it was, or some lingering scent of Keeshah identified it for her.

She cut a straight and destructive line through Thanasset's garden, then whined and crashed to the ground just as she reached the doorway. Lying on her side, she caught the stone sill with her forepaws and dragged herself into the dimness.

Keeshah followed, but Tarani remained with us, standing in the ruins of a flowerbed. I looked at her questioningly.

"It is Keeshah she needs now," Tarani said. "She is very grateful to be here."

A noise drew my attention to the street and the fence behind us, where three people—young boys—had expressed the crowd's curiosity by venturing in through the gate. Thanasset herded them out with dignity and good humor and spent a moment in the street, talking. When he came in and closed the gate, we could hear the sounds of people shuffling back down the street toward the business district of the city.

Thanasset walked back to us and said: "Welcome home, son."

I laughed and hugged him; he pounded me on the

back. I kissed Milda, picked her up, and whirled her around. The sweet old lady hugged me back and scolded me, laughing all the while.

I put Milda down and took Tarani's hand, suddenly at a loss for words. I wanted to tell them who she was, what she meant to me, what we had been through together, what we faced. What I said was: "This is Tarani."

Thanasset stared into Tarani's face. Then he did the odd and tender thing of lifting her free hand in both of his own and kissing the palm. "Our home is honored by your presence, Tarani," he said. "I am Thanasset, and this is Milda, sister of Markasset's mother."

"Welcome, dear," Milda said. "Come inside, please. You'll want some hot food, and then a bath."

Tarani followed Milda toward the house. Thanasset and I stood in the garden quietly for a little while longer, listening to the sounds of effort and pain and comfort coming from the brick structure.

"There is a story in this that I look forward to hearing," he said, with a smile. "When you are comfortable and rested. But I can wait no longer to hear the good news that you have brought the Ra'ira back."

I shook my head, and the tall man's shoulders drooped. I looked at Thanasset more closely and found him to be thinner, older, sadder than I remembered him.

How long have I been gone? I wondered, and quickly ran up an estimate of the time. *Four moons? Half a year? How could he have aged so quickly?*

"It's all the same story," I said, "and it's a long one. But Tarani and I have both pledged to deliver the Ra'ira safely into the hands of the Council, where its power cannot be misused."

"When?" Thanasset demanded sharply.

"I can't say, exactly," I answered.

"It must be soon, Rikardon," Thanasset said. "There is something you do not know about the Ra'ira—"

"But I *do* know what it can do," I interrupted. "I tried to tell you so in the letter I sent from Dyskornis—did you get it?"

"Yes, I received your letter." He pressed my shoulder. "It was thoughtful of you to send it, and foolish for me to have kept the entire truth from you." He hesitated. "I know you are weary," he said, "but would you mind walking a bit with me?"

I agreed, and we left by the garden gate to walk down to the marketplace. Thanasset said nothing, merely guided me and let me be shocked by what I had been too preoccupied to see while guiding Yayshah through the city. At that, the main thoroughfares we had traveled would have seemed little different from the city I had left. I might have noticed the disrepair of the mud-sealed stone pavement, but I would have assumed it was on the list of some foreman of a vineh paving crew.

Thanasset led me down side streets which were heaped with litter: fruit rinds, seeds, meat scraps that smelled as if they would soon be crawling with insects.

We stopped to watch a vineh street-cleaning team at work. Two of the pale-furred, apelike creatures swept up trash along the side wall of a square. Another followed, pushing a wheelbarrow. All three wore the slightly ludicrous shorts which somehow eliminated the natural and vicious rivalry between vineh males, which composed all of the city's maintenance crews. These three worked peacefully together, but they were supervised by two Gandalarans, rather than only one.

We walked for half an hour or so, covering a large chunk of the city, then returned to Thanasset's garden shortly before dusk. "I don't understand what you're trying to tell me," I said.

"You recall how the stone was guarded?" he asked, and I nodded. "A virtual cell, with a Supervisor in charge of it every minute of the day and night. That guard system was created by Serkajon himself, to insure that the Ra'ira would never be used to deceive and manipulate people again."

Thanasset paced through the growing darkness, holding his elbows. Sounds came from the sha'um inside the shelter, but Thanasset and the puzzle he was unravelling held my attention.

"One day a Supervisor discovered that the power of the Ra'ira could reach out to vineh," he said. "It had long been recognized that they had the native intelligence and the physical capability to perform simple tasks, but every attempt to train the occasionally captured individual had failed. This Supervisor reeled back from his first contact with a vineh mind—it was unrelievedly vicious. But he learned from that contact, and began to learn more. At a Council meeting while he was charged with care of the Ra'ira, he brought the stone and four male vineh into the chamber, explained to the startled and angry group that imposing docility on the creatures was a small-effort matter, and painted an eloquent picture of a city relieved of its menial chores."

Thanasset stopped and picked a leaf from a bush. "Since then, Rikardon, the Supervisors have not merely guarded the Ra'ira. They—we—have used it, watching the beastish thoughts of the vineh for signs of aggression and enforcing docility when necessary." He waved a hand in the direction of the street. "Some of the vineh are still tractable, as you saw just now. We think that must be the result of the long habit of obedience. But we have no faith that the habit will not wear off, in time, and even these few will join the wild ones that have spread across the hillsides west of the city, below the rakor mine."

He turned around and correctly read the expression I wore.

"I know it shocks you to learn that the Council is not as altruistic as you believed," Thanasset said. "Programs are under way to organize work crews made up of people; the problems of litter and sanitation in the city will be under control shortly. The real problem lies outside the walls. Our colony of 'tame' vineh was larger than any natural tribe could expect to get, and there are no wild tribes to compete with them for territory. The city will be surrounded shortly, and the outlying farmers will be at risk for their lives. We need the Ra'ira, Rikardon. Badly. And soon."

14

Someone screamed from the back of the yard. At the same time, a whining howl of pain sounded from inside the brick outbuilding. Thanasset and I followed the human sound. I burst through the door of the bathhouse to find Tarani wild-eyed and thrashing in the tile-lined tub. I splashed down beside her and wrapped my arms around her, her soapy skin getting grimy from my travel-worn clothes.

Milda's voice sounded from the doorway. "What is it?" she whispered. "What's wrong?"

"It's the female sha'um," I gasped, and checked quickly with Keeshah. He was frantically busy, guiding and helping and licking. He was excited, but not alarmed. "The birth has started."

"The girl is bound to the female?" Thanasset asked in amazement. "There are women who ride?"

"Only this one," I snapped, my hands busy trying to keep Tarani's elbows from cracking against the side of the tub. "Please, I'll explain it all later. We need some privacy right now."

"Of course," Milda said in her practical way. She shoved Thanasset out the door, and closed it quietly.

"Tarani," I said, "remember that you are *not* Yayshah. Come away from her, darling, your suffering can't help her." I sat up in the cool water and shook the girl's

130

shoulders, was relieved to see her eyes waver and focus on me for a moment before she threw her head back and screamed again.

I pulled her torso out of the water and into my arms, pulled her head around, and kissed her lips. She moved randomly for a moment more, not struggling, merely reacting to Yayshah's pain. She responded tentatively at first, then seemed to understand that I was offering her distraction.

By the time the sounds from the sha'um had quieted, Tarani and I had both bathed. Tarani wore the robe Milda had provided, and I wrapped myself strategically in the soggy towel. We left the bathhouse and walked up the path toward the back door of the main house, pausing to look toward the square building from which came only the sounds of suckling. Night had fallen, but the sky was moon gray and the yard filled with light and shadow from the house windows.

I put my arm around Tarani, and she leaned against me.

"Keeshah's as proud as if he'd given birth himself," I said. "And so am I—though I have far less reason."

"Yayshah is already asleep," Tarani said. "Do you think we might look in on them?"

I shook my head. "Keeshah's still fussing over the babies," I said. "We've waited this long—we can see them when we take breakfast to Keeshah and Yayshah."

"Thank you for being there when I needed you," she said quietly.

"My pleasure," I said, and won a true smile from her.

We went through the back door into the midhall of the largish house. The sound of the door closing brought Milda from the dining room on our right and Thanasset from the sitting room, close to the front door and on our left. Milda smothered a giggle and said: "I'll be serving a late supper—to people who are *dressed*."

"The sha'um—" Thanasset inquired.

"Everyone is fine," I said. "There are three cubs: two male, one female."

Tarani and I went upstairs. I found clean clothes laid out in my bedroom. Milda had prepared a spare room for Tarani, complete with a few wardrobe items. Tarani did justice to a beautiful gown and, in spite of having eaten lightly before her bath, to Milda's wonderful supper. I stuffed myself until I could barely move, then waddled into the sitting room and accepted a glass of barut from Thanasset.

Milda had disappeared at the first hint of "business." Having gotten to know the competent old lady both as Markasset and as Ricardo, I was fairly sure that she knew everything Thanasset did, but Milda valued the form of Thanasset's position as a Supervisor, and showed a public respect for his privacy.

Tarani accepted a glass of barut and listened silently to my recounting of everything—nearly—that had happened since I had left Raithskar. Most of it she had shared; some of it she had heard; a bit of it—in particular, my experience with Somil and Zaddorn in the All-Mind—was entirely new to her. Even as I started the story, Thanasset did not question her right to be present. When I had finished, he turned to her and unhesitatingly shared the secret so long withheld from me—the situation involving the vineh, and the imminent danger to the city.

Tarani looked at him sadly. "It would seem that the Ra'ira is nowhere safe from the misuse of men," she said. "I begin to think it should be destroyed."

Thanasset nodded. "That has been discussed within the Council," he said. "Our plan is to use the gem to guide the colony further west, to an area where there are wild vineh to provide them natural competition for territory and food, and then to dispose of the Ra'ira." He shrugged. "That plan is not universally accepted," he said, "but Ferrathyn is strongly in favor of it. He and I, with the support already present in the Council, should be able to convince those who want to resubdue the vineh into a work force."

"Who is Ferrathyn?" Tarani asked.

"The Chief Supervisor," I answered. "Is he well, Thanasset? The last time I saw him, he seemed to show his age more clearly."

"The strain of guiding the Council through this crisis has taken its toll on him, I am afraid," Thanasset said. "His body seems ever more weary, but his spirit is strong and vital. It is almost as though he gathers energy from adversity.

"I know he would have been delighted to hear this tale of a second sword and your search for Kä," Thanasset said, "and he would be moved, as I am, Tarani, to say that your effort in our behalf is deeply appreciated. Your commitment to leadership in Eddarta, and to the safe return of the Ra'ira, bode well for a return of good relations between our cities."

"Thank you, Thanasset." She put down her glass and stood up. The gown Milda had loaned her was inches too short, the sandals' soles far too wide for her delicate feet, yet she managed to look regal. Thanasset and I both stood up with her. "Rikardon has told me, in our few quiet moments together, of the beauty and comfort of Raithskar. I discounted some of his words as an expression of fondness for his birthplace, but I revise that opinion now. There is dignity and goodness here— errors, perhaps, as there must always be among men, but only sincere intentions."

"You speak of the city that produced Worfit," Thanasset said with a grim smile.

"I refer to the city which looks to the welfare of its people, and not to the profit of its rulers," she replied. "In all of Eddarta, there is no one, Lord or landservant, who can achieve that viewpoint. There *was* one who would have understood and appreciated Raithskar, but he died in Dyskornis."

Thanasset took Tarani's hand in both of his own. "You

133

have suffered much sadness and trial in your few years, Tarani," he said. "I hope you will regard this house as your home."

She smiled a little shakily, pressing his hands. "I believe I will say goodnight now," she said, and left the room.

"Tell me something," I asked Thanasset. "When you greeted Tarani in the garden—you didn't know she was bound to Yayshah as a Rider?"

"No."

"What you did—it was a very gracious, a very special greeting."

"Of course," Thanasset said. "How else should a father welcome the woman his son has chosen as a lifemate?"

"It's that obvious, is it?"

"It is that obvious," he agreed. He frowned. "It is also obvious that something is troubling you, Rikardon. May I help?"

"Only if you can help me find Kä," I said with a sigh. "The sword is important for what it can do toward getting the Ra'ira out of Eddarta," I explained. "But I believe it has another use. Do you remember the day you gave me Rika?"

Thanasset was quick to see what I meant. "Do you mean to say that Tarani is a Visitor, as well?" he demanded.

"I only think so," I admitted. "She doesn't even suspect it herself."

"How can that be?"

I laughed and slapped him on the shoulder, aware that I was ducking the issue once again.

"You might as well ask why Rika helped me remember," I said. "I don't know the answer to that, either."

The next morning, I went down to the marketplace early and purchased a side of glith, brought it back, and stood in the garden, calling Keeshah. Out of the sha'um house came a parade—Keeshah, the cubs, and then Yayshah. I heard the back door of Thanasset's house open

134

quietly, and I knew that Tarani, Thanasset and Milda were watching.

The cubs were well developed, with open eyes and good coordination. They were the size of full-grown leopards, but with thicker bodies, heavier legs, and a proportion problem that reminded me of the pups of large-breed dogs—their legs and paws seemed awkwardly large compared to the rest of their bodies.

The three kittens were not sleek, like their parents, but fuzzy. Their fur was longish and fine, and very pale. The little female's carried strong hints of darker, regular marking that resembled Yayshah's brindling, and by that evidence, I assumed the cubs would lose this "baby" fur somewhere on the road to adulthood.

I laid the meat on the ground. Keeshah paused to let the cubs move ahead. They sniffed at it, nipped delicately—their teeth were numerous and looked sharp, but were not fully emerged from their gums—then lost interest. Keeshah kept an eye on them while Yayshah attacked the glith meat. I was surprised that the adults did not drag the meat inside their house, then considered that it was probably cramped quarters in there for a family of five.

May I touch the cubs? I asked Keeshah.

Slow, the big sha'um cautioned me. *Have woman tell female.*

"Tarani," I called softly, turning back to the house. "Will you ask Yayshah if she will let me approach the cubs?"

The girl came down the pathway from the house, moving with a studied grace so as not to startle the sha'um. "I have asked her if *we* may greet the cubs," she answered. "She agrees—she is quite proud of them."

The cubs had wandered toward the garden. One of the males felt a branch of a bush touch his back, whirled to bat at it with a forepaw, and lost his balance. The flailing paws and tail attracted the other two, and in an instant there was a noisy melee of fur, rolling through Thanasset's garden. The cubs *sounded* surprisingly adult, and it didn't take long for the noise to disturb Keeshah.

He waded into the playful fight and started separating the combatants. The cubs had too much mass to allow for scruff-of-the-neck lifting, but the loose skin provided good purchase for dragging. Keeshah batted one of the males halfway to the bathhouse with one swipe of his paw, then grabbed the other male with his teeth and guided/forced it in our direction. The little female twisted to her feet and crouched with her ears and tail twitching, looking from one cub to the other. She barrelled after the unattached male and knocked him over. They rolled and squawled good-naturedly for a few seconds, then flopped down in a tangled ball of fur, panted heavily, and dropped off to sleep.

Tarani and I made friends with the cub Keeshah had brought us. The cub was unafraid and curious, sniffing at our hands and clothes, quickly acquiring Keeshah's fondness for being rubbed behind his ears.

Yayshah finished eating, and came over to us as Keeshah went to take his turn at the mass of raw meat and bone. The skin of Yayshah's belly sagged nearly to the ground, but it already showed signs of reshaping itself. The fur, which had looked patchy and thin across the distended skin, seemed darker and thicker now. Tarani went to Yayshah and stroked her; the female stretched out on the ground.

The cub I was playing with tired suddenly, and went to sleep with his head across my thigh. Just as suddenly, the other two cubs roused and, seeing their brother with a new toy, came to investigate. I had a moment's panic as I realized that I was momentarily pinned to the ground, and that most young predators "played" in ways that would train them to kill food—but the cubs had worn out their first burst of energy and were reasonably calm now. They nosed around me, accepting my touch and batting clawlessly at my arm when I offered it as a target, until they disturbed their brother. Then all three cubs seemed to notice Mama nearby and started nuzzling Yayshah's belly.

The female lumbered to her feet and led the kittens back into the dimness of the brick shelter. For the moment, playtime was over. So was breakfast. Keeshah jumped to the roof of the sha'um house and curled up to nap.

Tarani and I cleared away the glith carcass, then cleaned our hands and returned to the house. Milda had vanished into the kitchen, from which were coming the wonderful smells of a breakfast more appetizing than raw glith. Thanasset met us at the back door, put an arm around each of us, and hugged. His face sparkled with the same delight Ricardo might have expressed after watching a litter of domestic kittens at play. There is a special and tender charm about the young of any species.

"Sha'um cubs born outside the Valley," Thanasset said. "It is still hard to believe. Do you think Keeshah and Yayshah would allow me to get to know them?"

"I certainly hope so," I said. "I'll need to ask you and Milda to feed Yayshah and watch out for the cubs while we're out in the desert, looking for Kä."

"As to that," Thanasset said, drawing us across the midhall toward the door to the dining room, "you asked me for help in finding Kä, and I may have thought of something—"

"The desert?" interrupted Tarani. "Rikardon, the cubs have barely arrived."

"I mean to take only Keeshah, of course," I told her. "I think he will be willing to leave Yayshah and the kids with Thanasset—after all, this is his home."

"But it is not yet Yayshah's," she countered.

"She seems quite comfortable," I said, somewhat testily. Thanasset, wisely, had stepped back from his position between us and watched us in silence. "Thanasset can provide her with food, and the cubs will continue to nurse for a while. She will be all right without us."

"*Us?*" Tarani echoed. "I shall not leave her."

137

"I wouldn't ask it, under any other circumstances," I said. "But you know what's at stake here. The situation with the vineh—"

"Demands a greater speed than we anticipated, I grant you," the girl said, with a wave of her hand. "If Keeshah will leave Yayshah, you are free to begin the search. But I," she emphasized, "shall not leave her."

"You have to come with us," I said.

"If you both will excuse me," Thanasset murmured, "I will assist Milda with her kitchen duties." He escaped through the dining-room door; we hardly noticed his going.

"Why?" she demanded. "You have the Recorder's guidance, and whatever advice it is that Thanasset can offer. Two sets of eyes seem to be inadequate advantage to justify the strain on Keeshah of carrying us both into the desert."

She's right, I thought. *Logically, she's right. So now what do I say to convince her? I could tell her the truth—no, not now,* I convinced myself—too easily.

"For some reason, I have absolutely no confidence in being able to find that sword alone," I said. "Going without you doesn't *feel* right, Tarani—maybe because I think of that sword as yours, instead of mine."

She put her hands on her hips, walked away, looked back at me thoughtfully.

"In Thagorn, you *commanded* my movement, and Yayshah's," she said, "and I confess that, though I saw the worth in your judgment, I resented the tactic. But that pressure, at least, was clear and direct. I sense something else in your manner now, Rikardon; everything you say is true, but something remains hidden. You do not merely *want* me to go with you, you *need* my presence in some way—and I do not think it is associated with finding an ancient city."

She dropped her arms and came closer, searching my face.

138

"If you will tell me why you desire it so strongly," she said, "I will go with you."

I faltered, and for a moment fought desperately with the habit of concealment—but old habits are hard to break.

"I will tell you—when we reach Kä," I hedged.

"That does not meet the terms," she snapped.

"It is all I can offer," I replied, and grabbed her arm as she turned away. "Please believe me, Tarani—you *will* understand, when we find the sword. And it is very, very important."

She shrugged off my hand, took a step, turned back. "I will go," she said. Her voice made the words of consent sound threatening.

15

It was early afternoon of that same day. I was alone in the sitting room, looking over some old maps Thanasset had brought me from his office that morning. He had returned after lunch to continue searching for information about the ceramic pipeline that had once carried fresh water from Raithskar to Kä. I had no idea where Tarani was; she had left the house after breakfast with the stated intent of exploring the city. Milda had taken one of the lightweight armchairs and her stitchwork out into the garden, to watch the sha'um and discourage fence climbing by the local children, who were understandably fascinated by the presence of the cats.

Someone knocked at the door, and I set aside the map to go and open it. A smallish woman stood in the doorway, sunlight sparkling from drops of mist trapped in her golden headfur. She smiled at me uncertainly.

"Hello, Rikardon."

"Illia!" I said, truly pleased to see her. "Come in."

"I—no, thank you, Rikardon, I cannot stay. I heard that you had returned and that that—uh—there was someone with you. I only wanted to stop by and thank you for your letter."

She was looking somewhere past my shoulder. I touched her hand, and her gaze finally rested directly on my face. I smiled. "Please come inside for a moment,

Illia," I asked. "I'll be leaving again, soon—probably tomorrow. This may be our only chance to visit."

I tried to express the sincere welcome I felt, and the attempt was successful to the point that she smiled more naturally and nodded. I held the door for her, then showed her into the sitting room, cleared the maps from the table, and offered to ask Milda for some herb tea. Illia declined, and awkwardness threatened to take over again.

The girl had been Markasset's friend, actually his fiancee. Their relationship had been composed of one part physical attraction, one part her ambition to be the wife of the Supervisor she expected Markasset to be, and one part Markasset's need to feel appreciated. Illia had been present at the ceremony in which Thanasset presented Rika to me, and had learned, then, that I was a "Visitor" and that the Markasset she had loved was dead. She and I had spent some time together and discovered that the physical attraction lingered. We had made an attempt to "start over," but I could not merely be a replacement for Markasset, and we had soon realized that building the new connection would not be simple.

In Dyskornis, faced with the frightening knowledge of the Ra'ira's power, I had seen the impossibility of a "normal" lifestyle, and had written to the golden-furred girl with good wishes but a clear rejection of any relationship closer than friendship.

"How have you been—" I began.

"I hear Keeshah has a friend—" she said, at precisely the same time.

We laughed, and I started over. "I thought the news would be all over town by now," I said. "Keeshah has a *family*—his mate gave birth to three cubs last night."

She clapped her hands together. "Baby sha'um?" she said. "May I see them?"

"If they're outside, you can probably see them from the window," I said, and went to sit on the ledge that ran along the wall below the two tall, narrow windows. They were made of small, diamond-shaped pieces of glass fitted into a lattice-style frame made of small strips of wood. The frames were divided into two sections, and I opened the lower section of this window, motioning Illia to sit in front of me and look out.

One of the male cubs was just coming out of the sha'um house, using the instinctive stalking movement to sneak up on the female, who was propped unsteadily on her hind legs against the side of the brick building. She was absorbed in batting at Keeshah's twitching tail, which hung over the roof of the house, along with one hind foot. The tail was just within her reach—until her brother knocked her over.

The noise brought the other male on the run, and it was another three-way free-for-all. Keeshah stirred, lifted his head, growled, and relaxed again. Yayshah appeared from behind the building and tromped through the fight, dragging one of the males off and trapping him under a forepaw. She started licking him and he rolled over obligingly, nipping and licking at her jaw and neck as she cleaned him.

"She is beautiful," Illia breathed, touching my arm for emphasis. "And the cubs—Rikardon, this is a wondrous thing. How did it happen?"

The family scene seemed to have a special significance to me, with Illia sitting so close. Markasset's body had known hers very well, and continued to appreciate it. I stood up, trying not to be obvious about avoiding her touch.

"It has to do with—with the woman who came back with you," Illia said.

"Her name is Tarani," I said, "and yes, the female sha'um is hers. It's a long story that I've told too often lately. Besides, I want to hear about you. Are you still teaching? How is Zaddorn?"

"I am still teaching," she answered, then sighed. "As

142

for Zaddorn, his duties keep him well occupied. I suppose you've heard about the sickness."

"Sickness?"

"The worker vineh—there has been an epidemic of some sort. It spread quickly through the entire colony. They say the pain of it enrages the beast who has it, and that it lasts a long time. Most of the vineh tore their way through the confinement walls at the colony, and are roaming about the countryside. Zaddorn has nearly doubled his Peace and Security Force to provide guards along the roads and try to locate the vineh free of the disease, who simply wandered off because the way was open for them."

She paused, puzzled.

"Surely Thanasset mentioned this to you?"

"He did say something about trouble with the vineh," I hedged, "but to tell you the truth, we've been too preoccupied with the sha'um to think of much else."

So this is how the Council has explained the sudden hostility of the vineh, I thought. *I wonder if Zaddorn knows the truth.*

Illia stood up. "I really must go, Rikardon—I have tomorrow's lesson to plan."

I walked her to the door. "Give my best to Zaddorn when you see him," I said, "and take my greetings and good wishes to your parents."

She turned on the paving stone in front of Thanasset's doorway and smiled at me. "I am glad to have seen you again, Rikardon," she said. "And I do thank you for writing to me—it is only another sign of your thoughtfulness and honesty. If, as you say, you will be leaving Raithskar soon, I will say goodbye now."

She stretched up to kiss my cheek, and I reached down to hug her.

Tarani and Thanasset chose that moment to come walking up the street, arm in arm.

"Hello, Illia," Thanasset said, without embarrassment, but flashing me a quick wink to see he appreciated the situation. "May I present our guest, a traveler from Eddarta? Tarani, this is Illia, our good friend."

The two women presented startling contrasts—Illia short and golden, Tarani tall and dark-furred. Illia, in spite of a quick attempt to hide her reaction, looked at Tarani with the air of a competitor assessing an opponent. Tarani had natural poise and years of stage experience to help her maintain her composure, but her smile and verbal greeting to Illia were devoid of real warmth.

When Illia had hurried off down the street, I noticed that both Thanasset and Tarani were carrying bundles. They came inside the house and opened them—Tarani had been to the market to buy extra water bags for our foray into the desert, and Thanasset had brought home some dry and faded charts which he hoped would give me an idea where to start looking for the Raithskar end of the pipeline, if any of it remained to be found.

"I have this for you, as well," Thanasset said, sorting a fresher-looking sheet from the mass of old paper and handing it to me. "Ferrathyn was in his offices for a short while this morning. I took the liberty of speaking for you, Rikardon. I invited him to stop by and learn the results of your trip firsthand. I fear I teased him unfairly," he said, smiling, "with a description of Keeshah's family. He seemed intrigued, but complained of pain in his joints—indeed, movement seemed to cost him much effort.

"I provided him with a condensed report on your adventures and your current plans. He was startled and most regretful that you are leaving tomorrow, and that he would not have the chance to see you before you go, or to greet Tarani."

I opened the sheet—it was a letter from the Chief Supervisor, the cursive script precise and steady:

My friend—
    Please allow me to speak for the entire Council in appreciation and in apology. It was

our blind and foolish rules, born of the practice of deceit, that caused Thanasset's hesitation in confiding in you. From his account, a few words from him, before you last left Raithskar, might have saved you much distress.

Be kind enough to present my greetings to the lady Tarani, and express my hope of meeting her in the very near future. The good wishes of the Council go with her to Eddarta.

Raithskar is fortunate to have your strength and commitment in our service, Rikardon. You have the gratitude of a besieged city, and of its Chief Supervisor,

—Ferrathin

I handed it to Tarani, who read it and passed it on to Thanasset. When he had read it, Tarani said: "Please tell the Chief Supervisor that I also look forward to our meeting."

"Thank him for taking the time to write the note," I added, "and tell him I got the message. 'Besieged city,'" I quoted, laughing. "Subtle. Tell him we'll hurry."

The charts had given us information, but little real help in locating Kä. They had verified that a pipeline had indeed been built of expertly fitted ceramic tiles, and that it had taken water from the pool below the Skarkel Falls out toward Kä. But after Thanasset had worked for hours to decipher the badly faded notes, he had announced that the pipeline had *not* led all the way to Kä on the surface, but that channels had been cut and ceramic-lined in some areas, and natural fissures used in others.

The ground-based portions of the pipeline would be impossible to detect, but Tarani and I started our search west of Raithskar, looking for traces of the surface construction as a starting place. Keeshah, confident of Thanasset's devotion to his family, was looking forward to the trip—it seemed a long time since we had shared the exhilaration of a long run. Tarani had parted from Yayshah less happily, but had reported, grudgingly, that the female had protested less than the girl had expected.

I thought, privately, that Yayshah and Keeshah were both a bit glad of the promised few days' separation.

I had studied Thanasset's collection of maps to determine if the locations of Raithskar and Omergol had shifted much through the years, and concluded that they had not. Somil had defined Kä as equidistant from those two cities, and eight caravan-days away from either one. That translated to about six man-days for mapping purposes—a man-day was the approximate distance a man could walk comfortably in one day, allowing for meals and rest, which I thought of as roughly thirty miles. I had done some triangulation on several of the maps, and had a fair idea of the terrain to look for. I had already decided to spend a maximum of two hours searching for signs of the pipeline construction. After that, with or without that confirmed starting point, we would start southwest into the Kapiral Desert.

Tarani rode behind me on Keeshah, and both of us carried cargo in the form of sewn-hide bags strung together with thick ropes that rested across our thighs. I had a set of bags filled with dried meat and fruit, and another set which contained water. Tarani carried water bags, and we each had two smaller pouches fastened to our belts. Keeshah could carry us to Kä's approximate area in two days, and bring us back in the same time period. I had allowed for two days of searching, and brought along a sparing supply of food for Tarani and me for the full six days. Keeshah had fed well this morning and could go the entire time without eating again. He would be hungry, but he could survive.

Tarani and I were dressed for the desert, wearing tunics which hung loosely from our bodies but fastened securely at neck and wrists, and pants which tucked into mid-calf boots made of soft leather. The triangular scarves which would wrap our faces and heads when we really faced desert travel were presently tucked into our belts, along with extras to use as wet-cloths for Keeshah, when needed.

We were as well prepared as we could be—for the travel, at least. Tarani's deliberate silence nudged my guilt and prodded my anxiety. Whatever else happened on this trip, I knew I would be forced to share with Tarani the real truth—about me and about her. I looked forward to the relief of having it done with, but not to the uncertainty of its effect on our relationship.

Seeing Illia again had made me realize, yet again, how much challenge and complexity and grit there was to the woman who rode behind me—and how much I cared for her.

It was her sharp eyes which spotted the trace we were looking for, a ridge in a grain field that was too straight to be natural. We followed it southwest for a few minutes, then turned around to look. It lay along a straight line between us and the now-distant spot of whitish-gray that stood out against the darker gray of the cloud-crowned escarpment—the foot of the Skarkel Falls.

That brief look back nearly cost us dearly. Keeshah recognized the danger and sprang forward, even as his mind gave the warning: *Vineh!*

Tarani and I kept our seats through Keeshah's sudden lunge, but dropped to the ground by choice as the sha'um whirled to face the half-dozen apish creatures who had stalked us through the tall rows of grain. We threw aside our cargo, drew our swords and daggers, and moved well out to either side of Keeshah.

The vineh had spread out, as well, until there were two of them facing each one of us. Only with Keeshah were the odds sufficient to make the vineh hesitate. The others attacked.

The two I faced were full-grown vineh males, with hands as efficient as a man's and substantially better muscled. They were covered with pale, curly fur that cushioned blunt blows; unarmed, I would not have had a chance against them. The dual-edged weapons earned their respect quickly, however, and they backed away. The creatures were intelligent, and fully capable of a high degree of teamwork—we had seen a sample of that with the wild group we had encountered near Sulis. It amazed me that these creatures, so recently freed from the habit of docility and an artificial society, could have already achieved this level of group cooperation. It amazed me—but I had no time to dwell on it.

They came at me high and low, one tackling my legs and the other trying to grab and maim my sword arm—a fairly simple procedure, if it ever got its powerful, underslung jaw in range of any part of the arm. I twisted and brought the dagger across my body, into the side of the creature trying to get my arm. The wounded vineh gave a high-pitched, gurgling cry, and collapsed on the ground. I slammed down not far away, kicking at the vineh trying to bite a chunk from my leg. I stabbed with the sword; it connected, but not vitally. By rolling and kicking, I kept the vineh too off-balance to get purchase with its teeth, but it was slowly shifting its position to limit my movements, and the closest vulnerable area, its throat, was beyond my reach and shielded by its body.

I was starting to give way to panic when the vineh let go and shot upward, then bounced on the ground near its fallen companion. Keeshah was over him in an instant, his teeth fastened in the neck of the creature this time—and suddenly, it was over.

Tarani had come through the battle with a torn tunic and a few scratches; I had fared about the same. Keeshah's main loss was his composure; his mind seethed with battle fury and hatred for the vineh, and he spent a lot of energy in the next few minutes tossing the corpses around.

He did not, I noticed, eat the flesh of the vineh.

Tarani and I retrieved the bags, and discovered that one of the waterbags had been damaged.

"Do you want to go back for a replacement?" I asked.

"Can we manage without the water?" she countered.

"I think so."

"Then I say we drink what is left in this, and start our journey," she replied decisively. "We have seen evidence of the need for haste. And I am eager to have this task finished."

I agreed, and reached out for Keeshah mentally, trying to calm him. In a few minutes, we were on our way, running through the southwestern outskirts of Raithskar's farmland.

16

Finding Kä turned out to be the easy part of the trip. We soon lost, as expected, the guidance of the raised ridge, but Markasset's Gandalaran inner awareness helped me keep a fairly precise sense of direction. Common sense and a knowledge of Gandalaran technology—i.e., the lack of high-pressure pumping devices— would have delivered the conclusion that Kä had to be located at a lower altitude than the Skarkel Falls. The maps I had looked at—one of which I had brought along for reference—had provided enough detail about land formations to confirm that conclusion, and the physical features of the land conformed to what I expected.

The Skarkel River flowed southeast of the city, to interface with the Kapiral in a treacherous, salty bog. To the southwest, the land was less watered, and therefore less fertile. We soon left behind any trace of farmland and traveled through the gray, scrubby brush that somehow survived in the salty sand of the Gandalaran deserts.

Over the hours of travel, we realized we were following shallow, wide stairsteps—flat plateaus that led gradually downward. There was no wind, but our passing stirred up clouds of fine, stinging dust, and we wrapped our scarves tightly around our faces, leaving only our eyes exposed. It was not the first desert crossing the three of us had made together, nor was it the most difficult—but it was uncomfortable. Gandalara is always hot, but the reflective quality of the sand in the desert made it seem suffocatingly, blisteringly hot.

We slipped, without discussion, into the efficient travel pattern of moving for three hours, resting for one, allowing extra rest time for Keeshah when he asked for it. That cut our travel time by nearly a quarter, so that we reached what I judged to be the vicinity of Kä in midafternoon of our second day.

The land formations we followed had become more clearly defined, and we found ourselves approaching a ridge that marked the end of one of the long flat areas. Keeshah carried us up to it—and we looked down on Kä.

Tarani gasped and expressed the same thing I was thinking. "Surely it cannot be this simple," she said.

I shook my head. "We've found the city," I said, "but not the sword. When I shared memory with Zanek, I saw a huge room where he displayed the Bronze. It would have taken a big building to house that room, in the 'official' part of the city. Any suggestions?"

Kä was enormous. We had stumbled on the one specific vantage point that gave us the best view of the city. We dismounted, allowed ourselves and Keeshah a ration of water, then spent some time looking down on the seat of the ancient Kingdom.

"I do not understand," Tarani said. "The city is not 'hidden' at all—it hardly seems damaged by the passing years. Why has it not been located, and plundered?"

"We don't know that it hasn't," I said, "but if that happened, I'll bet it occurred just after the breakup of the Kingdom, when people still remembered, specifically, the wealth of the city. As for why nobody knows where it is now," I said, shrugging, "Who cares? There's nothing but desert beyond it. Even those mountains," I added, waving to the craggy foothills not far to the west, "are desert-dry. There is nothing here to bring people *past* Kä, to keep its location fresh in the All-Mind. If it

151

had a higher location, and were even faintly visible from the desert route between Raithskar and the Refreshment House at Yafnaar, it might still be popular with history students. But look at it—it's in a hole."

She did look. "Those buildings on the far side of the city—the regular grouping, do you see?"

I followed her pointing arm, and did see what she meant. There was a large center building and, radiating outward, a set of smaller ones. It was reminiscent of the arrangement of Lord City—further encouragement, since the Last King had been the one to lay out the construction of that settlement above Eddarta. The rest of Kä might have been transplanted from Raithskar. There was a large open area near the big building Tarani had noticed, and several smaller openings scattered around it. I presumed they served as Raithskar's did, as centers for specific business districts.

"I think you're right," I told Tarani. "Shall we go investigate?"

"We shall go into the city," she said, "and enter the first building which will provide shelter from the heat. You will tell me why it was so important that I come here with you. *Then* we shall seek out the sword."

I opened my mouth to argue, but simply closed it again.

"The time has come," ran the quote, remembered by Ricardo, through my mind, *"to talk of many things." In other words, she's right; I've run out of procrastination room.*

Keeshah took us down the slope below the ridge, which was less steep than it seemed, and through the streets of Kä. I had been correct in identifying the building material as stone, at least for the buildings we had seen from the ridge. Their walls were made of small sections of stone, not quarried smooth, but apparently selected and matched for size and color. Whatever had been used to cement the stones together had been designed for long wear—even after centuries, the rock showed more sand-scarring than the medium material.

There had been many more buildings in the city at one time, however. The land from the base of the ridge to the first stone building was heaped and pitted, and Keeshah found it difficult going until he located a smooth, straight stretch.

"We're on a street," I said, as the revelation struck me. "All those mounds are buildings that were made of *salt blocks*."

"Like the Refreshment Houses?" Tarani asked. "But those seem as permanent as stone."

"They are maintained," I explained, excitedly. "Surface scars can be patched with saturated salt mud, but the crystal structure will break down completely, given time, as these have done. The Fa'aldu can replace blocks when necessary, adding strength and life to the rest of the structure. These had no one to tend them, and eventually they just fell back into sand heaps."

"You speak of this, as you did of language, as if you have studied the destruction of cities," she said.

"Uh—" I replied.

She pointed. "There, a stone house. The roof is gone, but it seems large enough that the wall will shade us. We will stop there."

Remarkably little sand had drifted into the building—thanks, no doubt, to the stifling stillness of the desert air. Keeshah left us at the doorway, preferring the shade of an outer wall to the squeeze represented by the people-sized entries. As he curled up to rest, Tarani and I cleared away a mass of petrified wood pieces that must have been a dining table at one time.

We sat down in the wall's shade and I offered Tarani some food. She shook her head. "I am more hungry for truth," she said.

"All right," I said, after considering and rejecting softer ways to start. "I have been lying to you. I am not a 'Visitor'—not the way you understand it, anyway."

"But you are not Markasset," she said.

"No. I had another name, another life, in another *totally different* world, much bigger. My world had a pleth larger than all the land area, and rakor was so common that it was used to build cities larger than all the cities in Gandalara put together. The people of my world spoke many different languages."

She frowned, concentrating. "I find this—difficult to believe. There is no hint of such a time within the All-Mind."

"My world has no All-Mind," I said, and heard her catch her breath. "I learned about the past of my world through reading what other people wrote down, and by visiting cities like this, lost for centuries in the desert. My deserts were different, though, with constant winds that piled the sand so high that our ancient cities were buried under tons of soil."

She was silent for a long time, then suddenly snapped at me: "Why did you not tell me this at the beginning?"

"I was afraid you would not be able to believe me."

"You have said that strangely," she commented. "Not that I *would not* believe, but that I would be *incapable of* belief. You thought the truth would frighten me?"

"Yes," I admitted. "Doesn't it?"

"The strangeness of it disturbs me," she said, "but it explains many other things which have disturbed me more. For example—your ability to resist mindpower, which thinkers guess has some connection to the All-Mind. It seemed strange to me; I felt that merely having the two identities did not account for your immunity. If you were never a part of the All-Mind, then it is logical that a power associated with it would not affect you.

"I have always known that you *think* differently—with greater detachment, *sometimes* with greater logic," she said, her voice growing harsher. "I say 'sometimes' because I see no logic in your hiding this truth. Your deception has only created confusion and distrust. What did you gain by it?"

She saw me hesitate before I answered.

"There is more," she stated flatly. "Tell me."

"This part will be harder to believe," I warned her. She merely waited. "Just before I woke up in Markasset's body," I said, "I suffered a strange disaster in my own world. I can't begin to tell you what happened or why— but I *have* learned that the person who was with me also came to Gandalara. The person in whose body she appeared was still alive, and—"

"Enough!" Tarani ordered, and scrambled to her feet. I jumped up after her and grabbed her shoulders. She struggled, her eyes not looking at me, her mouth pressed into a tight, defiant line. "Let me go," she demanded.

I shook her and yelled at her, driven by anger and fear and the need to get this out into the open. "You can't ask for the truth and then reject part of it," I said. "There is a woman from my world in Gandalara; her mind and thoughts and personality *are alive in you*, Tarani. She has been influencing you in ways you can't really recognize. She might be helping you right now—*she* could be the reason that knowledge of my world doesn't frighten you."

"*No!*" Tarani screamed, and began to struggle furiously, but with no real intent to free herself—which surely saved me some bruises. I held on to her arms throughout the spell of activity, and she suddenly went quiet. She stood in front of me, panting, her fists tightly clenched above the wrists I held.

"How long has your friend been 'helping' me?" she asked in a low, vicious voice.

"I think—since Recorder school," I said. "You told me about a period of confusion, when you left the school. I think she came then, and you knew she was here, and part of the reason you have refused to use your Recorder skills is that it would remind you of that time. I think you have been afraid of her, Tarani—but she doesn't deserve your fear or hate. She had no more choice about this than you did."

"You truly believe there is another person inside of me?" she asked in that same quiet voice.

"I do. I—have spoken to her."

"And that she has 'helped' me—to debase myself with Molik, to bond with Yayshah, to—" She faltered. "—to learn to love you? That there is nothing in my life, since school, for which I can take responsibility, whether it be credit or blame?" Her voice had risen.

"Is it such a terrible thing to *understand* your past in this way, Tarani?" I asked. "She meant you no harm—"

"She—who?" the girl demanded. "Who is she? Who *was* she, to you, before you both came here?"

"Her name is Antonia," I said. "We had only just met when the disaster struck."

"Then how can you speak for her intent?" Tarani demanded.

I was losing patience. Resistance, I had expected—but jealousy? "I can't," I said. "Why don't you ask *her* what you want to know?"

Tarani became very still.

"Is that possible?" she asked.

"I think the sword can make it possible," I said, and released her arms. She lowered them and stepped back, seeming to cower against the wall. "Do you remember, in Dyskornis, that I asked you if my being a Visitor disturbed you? You asked if that wasn't the very reason why we were involved in this mess.

"Tarani, when I arrived in Gandalara, Markasset was dead. I didn't even have full control of his memories—until I touched Serkajon's sword. You have touched *this* sword with no effect. But there are two of us, and two of these swords."

"And you think the one left in Kä will release the one called Antonia?" she asked, the bitterness in her voice shocking me.

"I don't know what it will do," I admitted. "Your

156

situation is very different. But I *do* know that the two of you can't go on existing entirely separate in the same body. It's impossible to expect that your judgment won't be affected by Antonia—and, now that you know about her, by your suspicion of her interference. The sword may do nothing at all," I said. "But it seems to be the only possible key."

"This is the true reason you came in search of the second rakor sword," she said flatly. "Well, let us *find* the thing!"

She ran out of the building and down the roadway, heading straight for the large square in what we had guessed to be the government section of the city. I followed her with a goodly measure of panic troubling my breathing. We went into the biggest building and searched every room. Suggestion of the rich furnishings still remained in wall paintings, petrified wood carvings, and paper-dry bundles of tapestry, long since fallen from their hangers.

The sword was not there.

17

"Zefra said the sword was cast aside by the Last King in anger with the Sharith, as he was leaving Kä," Tarani reminded me. "If so, it would have remained in plain sight. It easily could have been stolen by profiteers."

"It was too valuable a thing in itself to be destroyed, and no one has heard of it since the last days of the Kingdom," I said. "It has to be here, still—somewhere."

Tarani leaned against a wall and crossed her arms. "Because your 'destiny' demands you be united with your friend?" she asked.

I threw down the crumbling tapestry I had just tried to move and turned to face her. "I want you to listen to what you just said: 'your' destiny; 'your' friend. Since when is this only *my* business, *my* need? In Dyskornis, we accepted a *joint* destiny, Tarani—and everything that has happened since has only brought us closer together, made us a more effective team."

She rearranged her position, but did not interrupt me.

"Antonia has been a part of that team all along," I said. "You haven't known about her—I didn't know about her for a long time. But she *is* here and, hard as it is for you to accept or even tolerate, she *did* guide your life toward our meeting point, though I doubt she was doing that consciously. I have given up speculating why this is all happening, and why, in particular, to us." That wasn't quite true, but such speculation was definitely a side issue to the point I was trying to make. "I just don't think it would hurt anything to make Antonia an active and visible part of the team.

"And yes, I *do* believe we are meant to find that sword."

She sighed. "How? It will take us days to search every building; we do not have that much time."

"You can find it," I said. "Or you can help me find it."

She put her hands flat against the wall, as though she were preparing to launch herself from it. Her arms were trembling.

"You mean to use me as a Recorder?" she asked.

"I think it is the only way to find the sword, Tarani. Don't you want to get this over with?"

"I do—more, perhaps, than you," she replied. "But you are correct about my reluctance to use the skills I was taught in Recorder School. The mere prospect of doing so frightens me terribly. It may be unreasonable, but the situation is unchangeable. I am sorry."

"What scares you about it, Tarani? The memories? It should be easier to face them now. Please, for your own sake, *please* try."

She stared at the floor, breathing hard, her entire body now trembling.

She's terrified, I thought, and began to have second thoughts about asking her to do this. It was too late; I had convinced her.

Her hands balled into fists and she moved determinedly into the clear center of the room—we had started and ended our search in the audience hall. "Come here," she ordered. "Quickly, before I change my mind!"

I ran to join her.

"I will have no success at all if I cannot become calm," she said. "I was taught a method—it will take a few moments of quiet. Say nothing until I speak again."

I nodded, and accepted her hand as we lay down together on the dusty stone floor.

She's putting herself into a trance state, I guessed as I heard her breathing become more quiet and felt her hand relaxing its deathgrip. *She is probably still terrified, though. This woman has been through enough,* I thought fiercely. *If she's got the courage to go through with this, it* has *to help her!*

Her hand tensed, and she laughed.

She sat up.

Antonia sat up, leaned over, and kissed me.

"This is what she feared," Antonia said, with her hand still on my chest. "To enter the All-Mind takes submission and self-release. She was doing this when I arrived, and that was the last time I had control."

The woman who was, and was not, Tarani stood up and stretched, then strolled across the room to touch a carved stone panel. I was too stunned to move, and I said the first thing that popped into my mind.

"You're speaking Gandaresh."

She laughed, Antonia's light rhythm sounding odd in Tarani's throaty voice.

"I see, *Dottore Carillo*, that you still practice your studies."

I stood up, beginning to understand what was happening, beginning not to like it much.

"Antonia, you know everything that has happened, don't you?" I asked her.

"Yes, Ricardo, I know. I have heard your truths and your lies, your talk of destiny. I have loved you—with *her* body."

She came toward me, touched my cheek with her hand. I marveled that the same flesh could change so dramatically with the mannerisms of a different personality. Tarani's presence was solid and competent, regal and elegant. Antonia gave off an air of less substantial power—sophistication, learning, beauty for its own sake. Her face was somber.

"You must help me, *Dottore*," she said.

"Whatever I can do," I said, puzzled. "As long as it won't hurt Tarani."

"Ah, there is the sadness," Antonia said, with a rueful smile. "I have indeed, as you suspect, influenced the life of this girl. But two things she has won on her own—the bond with Yayshah, and your devotion to her. I would share both, if I could," Antonia said. "But I know that, if you were forced to choose one of us, she would live and I would die a second time."

"Don't talk of dying," I said. "How can I help you?"

"You must help me accept the *possibility* of dying," she said, sadly. "For only then can I release this body to Tarani again, and let her find the sword. Ah, Ricardo, if you loved *me*, I would damn destiny and relegate the girl to the prison which has held me these long years. I cannot say it has not been interesting. I freely admit that existence in such circumstance was quite preferable to true death. But it is painful to have words that cannot be spoken, feelings that cannot be expressed. It is a trial to *influence* rather than *control*.

"This sword promises an end to it," she said. "But there is no telling what form that end will take. Serkajon's sword united you with Markasset's memories. Zanek's sword may purge Tarani of my presence."

"Surely—" I began. She put her fingers on my lips.

"Do not lie to me; the possibility exists," she said, and I nodded. "Then help me. Tarani is stronger than I; her courage astounds me. I believe she knew, when she began the trance, that I would emerge—and I *know* that she had no certainty that I would ever again relinquish control."

"Perhaps you don't have to," I said.

"Oh, but I must," she responded. "As Tarani pointed out, the All-Mind is Gandalaran—I could not act as a Recorder, even if the knowledge were my own and not second-hand. I did wish one more breath to be truly mine, and I felt a need to be close to you in my own body, even though it is a borrowed one."

I pulled her into an embrace and kissed her. Even that gesture was different under Antonia's direction—practiced and evocative, delicately sweet—but as sincere as Tarani's touch.

"Now," Antonia said, as she disentangled herself from my arms, "I will lie here again, and you will talk to me of the things which mean so much to Tarani. Speak of destiny or of Yayshah. Say anything about Gandalaran things, and I will let myself slip away."

"Antonia," I said, as she lay down precisely where she had been, and offered me her hand. I was too moved to say anything more; she seemed to understand, and squeezed my fingers.

"Talk to us, Ricardo. Hurry."

Gandalaran things, I thought frantically. *Zanek! Tarani has never asked for detail about what I learned in the All-Mind—probably because of the emotional load associated with Recording.*

I began to talk of the man I had met while I had been, physically, in Omergol with Somil. I talked of his ideals, the tragedy and loneliness of his life, of his commitment to a peaceful future. I described the years of daily decisions, their burden and satisfaction. And as I talked, a mood of kinship settled over me, as if I did not require the All-Mind as intermediary to visit Zanek. It was a feeling familiar to Ricardo in the ancient places of my other world—a connection made of time and curiosity, a sense of continuity and commonality.

Tarani's voice did not disturb the mood, but deepened it.

"Lie down," she said, and I obeyed. Our hands still touched.

"Will you seek?" she asked. The familiar timbre of power thrummed in her voice as, like Somil, she accepted the role of Recorder.

"I will seek, Recorder," I replied.

"Then make your mind one with mine, as I have made mine one with the All-Mind," she said, guiding our minds with the words.

"We begin."

I felt the same jarring wrench I had experienced with Somil, with the single difference that I had been expecting it, and we entered the brilliant vision of the All-Mind.

"*I am inexperienced,*" Tarani's mindvoice said. It was clear and strong, but impersonal, reprising Somil's sudden shift into ritual formality. "*Can you assist me in locating Kä?*"

I would not have thought so before she asked, but I knew I could. "*This way, I think, Recorder,*" I said, and we began to move along a shining cylinder—slowly, at first, then more quickly as Tarani became more confident.

After a moment, she spoke again. "*Yes, we are proceeding correctly.*"

I made no effort to verify that—both because I trusted her, and because my experience with Somil warned me away from it.

"*I see in your mind,*" she said, "*that you have some understanding of seeking. An object such as the sword cannot be our goal—rather, we must locate a lifememory with knowledge of the sword. It is my intent to seek out those who lived at the end of the Kingdom, and to share memory only briefly with several, rather than deeply with only one individual. Do you consent?*"

"Willingly," I said, remembering the pain of separation from Zanek. I did not care to suffer it again, and I did not want to put Tarani's Recorder skills to the test of dragging me out of the All-Mind against my will.

We sped ever faster along the glowing spokes. While the experience was similar to my search with Somil, there was a different quality to being with Tarani. I put it down to my already knowing Tarani, while Somil had been a stranger. I also wondered if Antonia's presence

163

had anything to do with it—I could sense no trace of the human woman's thoughts in the mind which carried mine through the shining network.

"*She is here,*" Tarani's mindvoice said, startling me. "*Even as you carry Markasset's memories within you, your friend lies within me.*" She must have sensed my surprise, for she continued. "*I do not know her,*" Tarani said, "*but I acknowledge her. I am aware of the choice she has made, and she was correct—if she had failed to relinquish all control, I could not have accomplished entry into the All-Mind. I am also aware that her eagerness for resolution is as strong as my own, and her uncertainty as great. She has won my respect.*"

We moved along in silence toward the center of the All-Mind, then slowed down and, as had happened with Somil, began to move along an arc of the sphere as Tarani scanned individual life memories for knowledge of the other sword.

"*I have located those who lived in Kä at the end of the Kingdom,*" she told me. "*This is not an ordinary seeking, in that seeker and Recorder both have need. It would be well, also, to limit our physical time as much as possible. Therefore, I shall share memory, and you shall view.*"

She did not ask or wait for my consent, but I would have given it gladly. Doing it this way gave me more detachment, so that the experience was even more like watching a film—a collage of well-directed character sketches.

We felt the fear of a court official, who was hastily packing up for the long march to Eddarta. He did not know about the Ra'ira; he merely knew that the slaves had stopped working, and that the Kingdom was finished. It was a credit to him that loyalty to Harthim was uppermost in his mind.

We labored with one of the workmen who removed the giant bronze sheet from its wall mounting and grunted under its weight, carrying it outside. We watched *it being mounted on a special sled-like arrangement equipped with vlek harness. We, too, felt anxiety about the coming change, and speculated whether we should move our wife and children to Raithskar. Would there be work?*

We were Harthim, and learned that Zefra's description of his handling of the sword had been correct. We lifted it from its place of honor in the audience hall, then threw it from us in disgust. A slave crossed the room to retrieve it, and we ordered him to leave it where it had fallen. We felt a deep sense of betrayal, remembering that we had admired Serkajon and sought his admiration, remembering—but not admitting—that we had loved him. We knew it was not Serkajon's act alone that drove us from Kä, but the absence of the Ra'ira. We felt crippled without it, suspicious of everyone, vulnerable as we had never been to the hidden thoughts of our friends and enemies, incapable of trust. We looked once more at the sword, then turned our backs on it.

We were the last person to leave the audience hall, on the day Harthim abandoned Kä. We were a slave, sent there to collect anything that might have been left, with the exception of the sword. We hesitated, calculating the value of the sword, but we recognized that discovery of such disobedience would mean death. We left it, in the corner against the wall.

Tarani paused, and skimmed along several cylinders. "There is no more here," her mindvoice said. "These people remember the sword, of course, but did not see it again. Harthim's leaving seemed to be a signal to which the entire city responded, and Kä was empty within a generation."

"Harthim left it on the floor of the audience hall," I said, "but it is gone now. Someone had to have moved it."

"Agreed," Tarani said. "It could have been anyone, at any time." There was true sadness in her mindvoice. "If we could trace places, as well as people, we might merely 'watch' the audience hall. Without that capability, I *believe that we cannot discover who removed the sword."*

I kept silent and thought hard. I was aware that Tarani was growing concerned about the passing of time, but I was still certain that we would find that sword, still hopeful that it would help Tarani. *If we are meant to find it,* I thought, *then I must know something to help us find it . . .*

"Serkajon!" I said. *"How did he know about the Ra'ira's power?"*

"I cannot say," Tarani replied. *"And I see no connection between that mystery and the sword."*

"There is no obvious connection," I admitted. *"But except for Harthim, Serkajon was the individual most involved in the end of the Kingdom. The sword and the Ra'ira were both symbols of power, and both are connected to Serkajon—the Ra'ira, because Serkajon stole it; the sword, because it represented the loyalty of Sharith to King, which Serkajon violated."*

Tarani hesitated.

"Serkajon," I pleaded. *"It can't take much time. If we don't learn anything—then I'll give up."*

She did not verbalize consent, but we moved along the arc once more. Without warning, we were Serkajon, skipping through his lifememory.

We were collapsed in the high part of the Alkhum Pass, struggling ever more weakly to breathe. We were thinking of the Valley beyond, imagining the pleasure of riding a sha'um. Suddenly, we thought of our father, and of his memory of us as one who had failed. We rallied against the vision, conserved our breath, began to crawl.

We led the Sharith cubs in a training exercise, and felt their unity and symmetry as an extension of ourselves. Everyone in the Sharith functioned as a part of the group, willingly shouldering part of the responsibility. We wondered why it could not be so in the Kingdom. We thought of the slaves who labored in the grain fields, tilling and carrying water to the dry earth that yielded less every year. We remembered the times we had walked with Harthim in his garden, and listened to him talk of government. He had made it seem reasonable and necessary, for the good of Gandalara, and we had been satisfied—until we rode through the fields again.

We began to move faster through the scenario that was Serkajon's lifememory. . . .

We became Captain. . . .

We tried to explain Harthim's policies to the Sharith, but were hampered by our own lack of understanding. . . .

We watched the slaves, and wondered how they could bear such a life. We saw one man explode with anger, dropping and spilling the precious load of water he was bringing from the reservoir, which had been filled from the Skarkel River. We watched him attack his supervisor, who stepped back and readied his sword. We watched him stop, shake his head, mutter an apology, retrieve his watersack, and turn back toward the reservoir. We puzzled over it, thinking that the man had acted as if someone controlled his thoughts. . . .

We understood. . . .

We were Zanek.

18

The shock of discovery jarred Tarani out of Serkajon's lifememory. *"Zanek returned as a Visitor to Serkajon's body?"* she said, her Recorder composure momentarily shattered. *"Surely if anyone had known that, it would be remembered in legend as well as the All-Mind."*

"Obviously, it was kept secret. But it explains why Serkajon knew about the Ra'ira's power. And if such a thing is possible at all, there is a definite logic to Zanek using the body and position of a man who was sympathetic to his own ideals."

Tarani recovered, and plunged us back into the lifememory that had been assumed by Zanek.

We were surprised to be once again in the world, but we quickly understood that we were needed. We kept ourselves hidden, and wore Serkajon as a mask against the Ra'ira's power. We were curious that Harthim saw the Captain's discontent, and addressed it with words, but that he made no effort to control it. Once, in the King's presence, we used the Ra'ira to see Harthim's thoughts.

From that moment, we no longer hated the King, or despised him for the way in which he ruled the Kingdom we had created. Harthim was acting only according to his training. He had been raised amid dissatisfaction and distrust, for which we bore more charge than Harthim.

We had exercised our vision shortsightedly. Had we not placed Kä at the edge of the Great Pleth, even though we had been the one to perceive that the deserts were growing because the pleths were shrinking? Those who followed us as Kings had been loyal to our vision, but blind to our failing. As the lifegiving water of the Great Pleth had retreated through the years, sustaining Kä had become a heavier burden. Now it stood isolated in desert, its continued life bought at a terrible cost.

We saw that Harthim recognized in Serkajon an integrity and sense of purpose that was missing in his own friendless life and that, in a pure and true sense, the King loved his Captain. He wished to believe his love and loyalty were returned; Harthim never tested Serkajon with the Ra'ira.

We did not hate Harthim, and we wasted no guilt on ourselves, but resolved to act. The Kingdom was useless as it now existed; what we had created, we would destroy. We became a thief, and abused the Ra'ira ourselves in pressing sleep and forgetfulness upon Harthim when he discovered us.

We took the Ra'ira to Raithskar, and threw it into the forge fires of the rakor foundry. The treacherous jewel emerged unharmed. We realized that the power of the Ra'ira was more dangerous in secret, so we called the best leaders in Raithskar and tested them. To those men alone, we revealed the secret of the Kingdom's power, and we pledged them to keep it ever safe from such use.

We skipped through the period still remembered in Raithskarian and Sharith legend, when the Riders had abandoned Harthim. I was curious as to whether Zanek had used the Ra'ira's power to influence their decision, but I was willing to leave that curiosity unsatisfied.

We were back in Kä, some years later. We went to the audience hall, and viewed the wall where the Bronze had been mounted. The wall was broken in several places; removing the mountings had been no simple task, and had left sections of stone shattered. We remembered the

Bronze and its message, and regretted that it had been so poorly heeded.

We wished a silent and personal farewell to the Kingdom, and turned away. Our foot struck a fallen tapestry, and we stumbled. We lifted the weaving to study it—and rakor gleamed beneath it. Harthim's sword, discarded during the King's flight, had lain here all this time, providentially hidden beneath this torn and worthless wall hanging.

We lifted the sword and mourned, for ourself and for Serkajon, the shattering of our bond. We knew the value of the weapon, but we also knew its history. It had been the King's sword, as potent a symbol as the Ra'ira, and we thought it best that this symbol, too, should disappear from sight.

As we looked about the room, we noticed the broken areas of the wall, and went to investigate. The wall was thick, built three stones deep, so that the breakage had only affected the first layer, creating depressions no deeper than two hand-spans—far too shallow to admit the sword. There were two entire surface stones missing, separated by a section of rock still intact. The pattern of three would have been directly under the lower left corner of the Bronze.

We used a heavy piece of rock to break up the remaining stone, and cleared it out of the wall. We pressed the sword of rakor into the long vertical opening; it lodged securely. Then we began to repack the opening with chunks of rock, flatter stones held in place with sharper-edged pieces. We pounded the covering when it was finished, to even the surface slightly and to force the outermost edges of the mass into what mortar still clung to the boundary stones.

We stepped back to survey the work. The patching could not be mistaken for a part of the original wall, to be sure, but its placement made it less noticeable, and we felt the sword was well concealed from any but a knowing search.

We felt a rare and clean sense of satisfaction, and a dawning peace. We realized that the task for which we had returned was complete.

We were Serkajon once more. We remembered all that Zanek had done, and approved. We left Kä, and considered it truly abandoned.

Tarani pulled me away from the lifememory of Serkajon/Zanek, and we sped dizzily through the tangle of glowing cylinders to the edge of the sphere. She had to pause there to soothe her excitement and eagerness into the measured calm of a Recorder. In a moment, she said: *"I shall withdraw our minds from the All-Mind."*

The brilliant glow faded into darkness, and I felt union with my body again; it felt stiff and awkward.

"And mine from yours," Tarani ended the ritual, and I was alone.

I sat up and started rubbing my arms and legs with hands that took their own sweet time in becoming responsive. My inner awareness and the dimmer light in the room told me it was late afternoon, and the relative speed with which feeling was coming back to my flesh confirmed it was the same afternoon in which we had entered the All-Mind. Tarani and I had been "gone" from our bodies only a few hours.

Tarani's eagerness—or determination—sent her crawling toward the back wall of the chamber as soon as she woke. Her movement was clumsy at first, but soon became more efficient. I stood and followed her.

The vertical patch of smaller stones was very close to the floor, and seemed to rise from the other rubble piled around its base. I had seen the place on my first look around the room, and had merely assumed that the top of the pile had fallen in a peculiarly vertical arrangement.

Tarani and I cleared the rock fragments from the base of the wall and began to pry and pull at the small rocks. A few came free in our hands; a few more could be worried

171

out with our daggers. It seemed as if an eternity had passed while we knelt there, but it really took us only a few minutes to move the stones that *would* move.

We had opened small areas at the top and bottom of the patch, but the center of it was effectively blocked by a large flat stone wedged in between the original stones at either side. Its strong purchase served as an anchor for most of the smaller stones above and below it. Neither of the openings we had made were large enough to admit a hand, and it would clearly be impossible to maneuver the sword out of the opening with that center stone still in place.

Tarani glanced at the doorway of the room, which was the only source of light—the room beyond seemed to be a reception hallway, with many windows, but the audience hall would have needed constant lamplight. It was perceptibly more dim in the room now, and my inner awareness told me we had very little time until dark. This room would be pitch black, and with all our other planning, we had brought nothing with which to make light—not a lamp, not a candle, not even a sparker (assuming we might be able to find something burnable in this ruined city). Fires were unnecessary as a source of warmth, and we had packed dried or long-lasting food for the journey. A sha'um could run even through the moonless darkness, guided as well by his sense of smell as by his eyesight.

Tarani turned back to me, her face tight and strained. "Rikardon, I do *not* wish to spend the night in speculation."

I nodded, and edged her out of the way. I put the blade of my bronze dagger into the upper opening, braced it and pulled, trying to break the tension of the covering rocks by forcing them outward.

The dagger snapped.

It was perceptibly darker in the room.

I drew Rika, and put its point into the opening. It was conceivable that the edge might be dulled against the

172

rock, but the tempered steel promised the capability of applying more pressure. The opening was awkwardly shaped, and the lever advantage of the sword severely limited by the proportions of blade inside and outside the concealing hollow.

I braced the point of the sword and pulled. A few stones dislodged, skittering to the floor around my feet. Their leaving enlarged the opening slightly, and another effort cleared away most of the smaller rocks above the flat center stone. I could put my hand inside and touch the blade of the sword, but my fingers could not grip it. The opening was placed where blade met hilt on the concealed sword; the hilt itself was still blocked at the uppermost area of the patch.

I removed my hand, and slipped Rika's blade through the opening, forcing it as far down into the hiding space as it would go. I was satisfied that outward pressure, now, would apply directly to the retaining center stone.

Tarani, who had watched me work, now joined me at the wall, and our four hands found secure purchase on Rika's hilt or on one another.

We pulled together, grimacing against the strain. I was afraid that even the tempered steel would break, but it held, bending slightly.

Nothing moved.

We caught our breath and pulled again. This time, we were encouraged by a small grating sound.

We had light and energy left for one last try, and Tarani and I prepared for it carefully. I held Rika's hilt and helped support her weight as she swung her legs off the floor. She braced her feet against the wall on one side of the stubborn center stone. When she was in position, I placed my left foot against the wall on the other side of the patch, directly opposite her feet.

We pulled, expressing the cost of the effort in a grim, moaning sound.

The stone hitched, moved again, then let go. I heard it crash and slide on the fragment-littered floor as I was doing the same thing, several feet away from the wall. Tarani had flown even farther across the room, but we both scrambled back to the patch and worked furiously to clear away what was left of the lower covering.

When it was done, I waited for Tarani to reach into the hiding place and retrieve the sword. She knelt beside me in the dust, her hands flat against her thighs. It was nearly dark, but I could follow her movement as her hands moved toward the opening and stopped.

"Not in the dark," she said suddenly. "Rikardon, bring it outside, into the clean air." Without waiting for my consent, she stood up and ran for the dim gray rectangle that was the door of the room.

I reached in at the freshly cleared base of the opening, which was at floor level, and worked my fingers carefully around the still-sharp edge of the sword. I pulled at the point until it scraped forward. Guided now by touch rather than sight, I jockeyed the steel blade until the point emerged from the wall, then rocked and turned and twisted and pulled until the hilt came free of its encasement.

I put Rika back through my baldric, and walked cautiously across the rock-strewn floor, carrying the Sword of Kings. My hands had tingled when my fingers first had touched it, but there was no special sensation now, and I attributed that earlier reaction to the memory of Rika's effect on me.

What will this do to—or for—Tarani and Antonia? I wondered.

Tarani was waiting for me in the huge square that fronted the audience hall. Diffused moonlight provided fair lighting, though shadows were deceptive and perspectives slightly altered by the silvery quality of the light. This place was very similar to Raithskar's main square, with stone pavement and an occasional bench. I laid the sword down on one of the benches.

"There it is," I said. "What we came for."

"For different reasons," Tarani amended. She stood on the other side of the bench, her hands pressed tightly together in front of her. "Did you ever believe in my reasons?" she demanded.

"Yes and no," I replied. "I believed what you told me, that the sword existed and that you needed it as a tangible symbol of your right to rule Eddarta."

"But you did not believe—" she prompted.

"You know what my reasons were," I said. "I was never sure that you weren't working, subconsciously, for my goal, and that the political value of the sword wasn't merely a rationalization."

"You mean you thought the *other* was moving me," Tarani exploded, "and I was searching for a logical reason for my actions."

"Yes, that's what I mean," I snapped, then drew several deep breaths. "Tarani, anger won't help either one of us," I said at last. "What bothers you more— knowing that someone else has lived inside you and guided you? Or not knowing *her* and how she can affect your actions?"

"Both things trouble me," Tarani said, "but not so much as the knowledge that you knew her, that you know her now, and that *you did not warn me of her presence.*"

"I accept fault in that, Tarani. It was fear that kept me silent. To tell you about Antonia, I had to tell you the truth about myself and make you aware that I had lied to you. Your trust and faith are precious to me, and I was afraid to risk them. I knew, too, that knowledge of Antonia would disturb you and make you distrust yourself. When I first learned about Antonia, I could not offer you even the hope of ending the duality."

"When you learned—" she echoed. "When *did* you learn about her?"

I hesitated.

"Rikardon? No more deception."

"I had no idea she was here, until we arrived in Eddarta. There was a moment when we were very close. . . ."

"And you turned away," she said, her voice suddenly gentle and sad. "It might have been best to tell me then—it could have caused no deeper pain."

"I was shocked, and confused," I apologized. "I was just beginning to see what Antonia's hidden presence must have meant to you."

"How did you recognize her?" she asked.

"She called me by the name I carried in that other world," I said, then shrugged. "Tarani, what is the point of all this discussion?"

"The point is," she began angrily, then stopped. "Rikardon, I am frightened. I believe I can pinpoint the other times at which the one called Antonia has spoken to you. They were moments of passion, words of caring, were they not?"

I nodded. "Until she appeared just before we entered the All-Mind," I confirmed.

"Knowledge of her has given me more understanding," she said, walking closer to the bench. "Outside of Thagorn, when I cried out with all my voice and mind against the frustration and loss and despair I have suffered, I know now that I was expressing *her* frustration, *her* loss, *her* despair, as well as mine."

She gestured toward the sword. "I, too, desire the oneness you say this sword *may* give me. I do, desperately, wish for an end to the uncertainty about what touching the sword *will* do. But before I commit myself to whatever change may occur, there is one more truth I must know."

"Ask it," I said.

"The caring we have shared, you and I. Is—is any part of it truly mine?"

"All of it," I said. "I admit to being unsure on that point, myself, for a while. But I am sure now." I went

176

around the bench to be close to her. I touched her face, nearly at a level with my own. "If you and Antonia become blended to any degree, you will *know* that I love you, Tarani—because she knows it. I can only tell you so, and your believing it depends on whether I have totally destroyed your trust."

She came into my arms and held me tightly for a moment, pressing her face into my shoulder. Then she stepped away.

"I do believe you, Rikardon," she said. "And I think more gently, now, of your friend, for the person you care for would not exist, but for the changes she wrought in my life. Will you—"

Her voice failed, and she pointed a trembling hand toward the sword. I lifted it by the blade, and offered her the hilt. She took it in both her hands.

A shock ran through her body, stirring my memory of Thanasset handing me Rika, and the peculiar sensation of learning everything about Markasset in one crashing, overwhelming instant. She staggered back a few steps, her hands clenching the sword hilt. Then she fell to her knees, dropped the point of the sword to the pavement, hunched over, and began to sob.

I knelt beside her and put my arm lightly around her shoulders. She seemed not to notice me, and I merely waited until her breathing slowed. Finally, she lifted her head and looked at me.

I searched her face for change, and could find none. She smiled, a tender and wavering curving of her lips, and moved her feet. I helped her stand; she sagged against me and my concern mounted.

"Sit here," I said, leading her to the bench. "I'll bring the water sack, and some food."

Her hand on my arm held me beside her.

"That will be most welcome, in a moment," the girl said. "We have ignored the needs of our bodies, following our visit to the All-Mind. But do not look so

177

stricken, Rikardon—it is only fatigue which weakens me."

I could not contain the question any longer.

"Who are you?"

"I am Tarani," she said. "Antonia has gone, but she has left behind her memory and understanding of your world—*Ricardo Carillo*."

I drew her hand down my arm until I could hold it. "That person exists *only* in memory," I said. "I am Rikardon now."

"Her memories are too many, and too strange, to bear close examination now," Tarani said.

I nodded. "It was that way for me, too. Markasset is still a stranger to me in many ways."

Tarani rested her head on my shoulder. "I met Antonia for a brief instant," she said. "I suspect it was her choice, because she wanted me to understand that she did not regret the need of her going. She truly loved you, Rikardon, wholly and separately from my feelings. Yet there was no bitterness in her for my winning your love—only the kindest wishes for our happiness."

I tightened my arm around her shoulders, moved by the wistfulness and wonder in her voice—moved, too, by the basic goodness I had seen in my brief association with Antonia, which was now lost to both of us.

"I would weep in sadness for her and gratitude, if it were possible," Tarani said. Then she lifted her head, smiling with more spirit, and a trace of mischief. "But in Raithskar there is a large 'cat' who wants me to play with her 'kittens.'"

We both laughed, then she grew serious again and looked down at the sword in her hand.

"In Eddarta, there is a danger to be controlled."

The thoughtful mood passed from her quickly.

"It was whispered in Recorder School that the infamous Somil used a rather unorthodox method to restore his energy after a session. Tell me," she said lightly, "is that true?"

"I can't speak from personal observation," I said, "but it seemed likely. I think your real question," I added, taking the sword from her hands and replacing it on the bench, "is whether his method is effective.

"Shall we test it for ourselves?"

END PROCEEDINGS:
INPUT SESSION FIVE

—*I have withdrawn our minds from the All-Mind . . . and now I withdraw mine from yours . . . was the session as painful as you anticipated?*

—*Yes. But I believe, in making this portion of the Record, that I have finally freed myself from the guilt I felt over deceiving Tarani.*

—*Be consoled by her own statement, that she could not have been herself without the hidden presence of your friend.*

—*It is true of us all, I believe, that we are shaped by our choices and circumstances.*

—*You are sad. Why?*

—*Antonia.*

—*Your grief honors her. But now, you must rest. You will be needed at the close of the festival. When time permits, we will continue the Record.*

ABOUT THE AUTHORS

RANDALL GARRETT, a veteran science fiction and fantasy writer, and VICKI ANN HEYDRON, a newcomer to the field, met in 1975 in the California home of their mutual agent, Tracy E. Blackstone. Within a year, they had decided to begin working together and, in December 1978, they were married.

Currently, they are living in Austin, Texas, where they are working on the Gandalara novels, of which *The Steel of Raithskar* is the first, *The Glass of Dyskornis* second, *The Bronze of Eddarta* third, *The Well of Darkness* fourth, and *The Search for Kä* fifth.

Coming in the spring of 1985 . . .
The sixth volume in the stirring science fiction series
THE GANDALARA CYCLE

RETURN
TO
EDDARTA

by Randall Garrett and Vicki Ann Heydron

Armed with the second steel sword, Tarani and Rikardon plan to head secretly back to Eddarta to lead a political coup against the High Lord.

Read RETURN TO EDDARTA, on sale in the spring of 1985, wherever Bantam paperbacks are sold.

WEST
of
EDEN

by
Harry Harrison

Sixty-five million years ago, a disastrous cataclysm exterminated three-quarters of all species on earth. Overnight, the age of the dinosaurs was ended; the age of the mammals had begun. But if that disaster had never happened and the dinosaurs had survived to fulfill their evolutionary destiny, this is what the world might have been. The world WEST OF EDEN.

A fascinating and deeply moving saga of two cultures fated to struggle for control of the earth, WEST OF EDEN is a remarkable odyssey, a scientifically accurate projection of what could have been the true history of our world.

Buy WEST OF EDEN, on sale now wherever Bantam hardcovers are sold, or use the handy coupon below for ordering:

A SEARING NOVEL BY THE AUTHOR OF
ESCAPE FROM NEW YORK

JITTERBUG
by Mike McQuay

2155 A.D.: America is ruled by a fanatical Arab dictator with life-and-death power over every human being on earth. His weapon of control: the Jitterbug—a devastating plague used as an instrument of genocidal extermination. In the cities, the only refuge, millions of people struggle for survival while a ruthless cabal of amoral executives battle each other for the remnants of power. Out of the Southwestern desert comes Olson, an outlaw and outsider. Aided by blind chance, and a woman who knows the corporation's darkest secrets, he dares to challenge its corrupt rule. Only his strength can stand against the tide of destruction. Only his courage can make a better world out of the chaos of the old.

Read JITTERBUG, on sale July 15, 1984, wherever Bantam paperbacks are sold, or use the handy coupon below for ordering: